ON A DARKLING PLAIN
Stories from the Great Depression

Betty Jean Tucker

Livingston Press
The University of West Alabama

Copyright © 2014 Betty Jean Tucker
All rights reserved, including electronic text
ISBN 13: 978-1-60489-130-0, hardcover
ISBN 13: 978-1-60489-131-7, trade paper
ISBN: 1-60489-130-0 hardcover
ISBN: 1-60489-131-9 trade paper
Library of Congress Control Number: 2014932119
Printed on acid-free paper.
Printed in the United States of America by
EBSCO Media
Hardcover binding by: Heckman Bindery
Typesetting and page layout: Emily Edwards, Amanda Joy Nolin
Proofreading: Joe Taylor, Emma Kay McClung, Verdie Coleman III,
Angela Brown, Amanda Joy Nolin, Tricia Taylor, Warren Enriquez, Breanna Black
Cover design and layout: Emily Edwards, Emma Kay McClung
Cover artwork: Ruby Pickens Tartt, courtesy of Jim Williams

Some of these stories were previously published in *The Montevallo Review, Alabama Prize Stories 1970, Belles' Letters: Contemporary Storeis by Alabama Women, Alabama Bound, Ball State Forum, Alalitcom*, and *The Token*.

With two exceptions, the people, places, and events in these stories are fictional. In "Bless Her Heart," the character of Maggie's great-grandmother (*not* her grandmother, Faith Baldwin) was inspired by the author's great-grandmother, Nancy Davis Hall, who was indeed the niece of Jefferson Davis. In "The Legacy" the story of Rube Burrows' life and outlawry and the town of Linden are factual. I am grateful to Howard Reeves, editor of the *Lamar-Democrat*, for permission to use the Rube Burrows' material from Joe Acee's book *Rube Burrows*, which was published in a revised edition in the 1989 by the *Lamar-Democrat*.

Grateful acknowledgment is made to the following: Norman McMillan, Wayne Flynt, the late Mary Ward Brown, Sylvia Gilmore, Wynell Stokes, Allison Brantley, Kimberly Poorbaugh, Jake Lill, And Maleah Digmon. I am especially grateful to Joe Taylor and the Livingston Press staff for giving *On a Darkling Plain* a niche in Southern literature.

This is a work of fiction. Any resemblance to persons living or dead is coincidental. Livingston Press is part of The University of West Alabama, and thereby has non-profit status. Donations are tax-deductible.

first edition
6 5 4 3 2 1

ON A DARKLING PLAIN
Stories from the Great Depression

On a Darkling Plain is for my children, Ken and Trac, and for my grandchildren, Corey, Jake, Allison, Kimberly, Lara, Rachel, and Maggie Grace, all of whom make sure that the landscape of my own life is not a darkling plain.

And in memory of my mother, Adelle Foxhall, and all the others who slogged through the Great Depression to survive and to keep dreams alive.

Table of Contents

Introduction to On a Darkling Plain	i
When Poets Lie	1
The Taboo Factor	32
The Dog That Wasn't a Dog	46
A Bunch of Blueness	53
The Renaissance Man	65
Hungers	91
The Poet's Deer	108
Bless Her Heart	122
The Legacy	132
Callie	151

Introduction to *On a Darkling Plain*

In 1951, a gifted nineteen-year-old student at Alabama College named Betty Jean Foxhall—the Betty Jean Tucker of this collection—published a short story, "My Sister Callie," in the *Montevallo Review*, a literary journal founded by the eccentric and prolific author Robert Payne, who by chance came to teach at Montevallo in the early fifties. The story was good enough to be chosen as one of the one hundred most distinguished short stories of the year by the noted anthologist, Martha Foley, and an even greater accolade came when the distinguished American poet William Carlos Williams, after reading the story, wrote this to his friend, Robert Payne:

> Betty Jean Foxhall's story is brilliant. I don't know how she can miss doing outstanding work if only she can avoid selling herself to the commercials—but that is a big if. They will be after her and the temptation is frequently overwhelming. Well, I wish her luck. She must not 'omit' her *self* at their instigation.

As it has turned out, Williams had no reason to fret, as in the many years since he sounded that word of caution Tucker has never been tempted to write for slick magazines. In fact, all of her fiction might properly be called literary fiction, a quality illustrated by Tucker's alluding to Matthew Arnold's "Dover Beach" in the title of this collection, *On a Darkling Plain*. The metaphor, which applies to all the stories, is found in these lines from the poem:

> For we are here as on a darkling plain
> Swept with confused alarms of struggle and flight

The stories in *On a Darkling Plain* have been written over six decades. Five of them have been published over the years; five have not been published. Four are prize-winning stories. That Tucker accomplished all this while working full-time as a journalist and teacher speaks to her sustained commitment to the craft of writing.

All of the stories in *On a Darkling Plain* are either set during the Great Depression or look back to that period, and they all take place in Alabama's Black Belt. Betty Jean Tucker was born in the Black Belt during the Depression, and she has lived almost all of her life in Linden, Alabama. Her profound knowledge of this part of the world and her deep understanding of the people who struggled to survive in that difficult time provide the foundation on which these stories rest. Others — John Steinbeck, Erskine Caldwell, and Eudora Welty, for example — have written about the Depression, and I would comfortably place Tucker's intimate knowledge of the period alongside that of those prominent writers. She says somewhere that "the Depression left its DNA of hungers and heartaches on the heart of history," and I think that only someone with a deeply-felt knowledge of this DNA could have written the stories in this collection.

It has almost become a cliché that the best fiction grows out of a deep sense of place. In her classic essay on the topic, Eudora Welty says the following:

> I think the sense of place is as essential to good and honest writing as a logical mind; surely they are somewhat related. It is by knowing where you stand that you grow able to judge where you are. Place absorbs our earliest notice and attention, it bestows on us our original awareness; and our critical powers spring up from the study of it and the growth of experience inside it. It perseveres in bringing us back to earth when we fly too high. It never really stops informing us, for it is ever astir, alive,

changing, reflecting, like the mind of man itself.
Betty Jean Tucker has found in the Alabama Black Belt the golden thread, as Welty describes it, that anchors her as a writer.

The Great Depression provides the sort of tensions that are the age-old stuff of good stories. The extreme economic circumstances of the period spill over into every aspect of life, offering sharp possibilities of conflict and survival. The tendencies to hate or to love, to fear or to trust, to hurt or to help, to despise life or to value it — all are magnified dramatically in the heightened world. Tucker understands all this, and she is quite willing to explore this world with grit, grace, courage, and a total lack of sentimentality. She does not shy away from a world replete with violence of all sorts — murder, suicide, other violent death, marital rape, bigotry, and terrorism. Religion, which is often regarded as a comfort to the oppressed, is of little solace to the characters in these stories. Tucker also looks unflinchingly at the racism of the period, and she describes the horrors of abandonment so common in those difficult times.

The historian and author Wayne Flynt, after reading these stories, pointed out quite correctly that the stories, though set in what may seem the far-off past to some readers, will most assuredly resonate with modern readers. He says the following:

>...to American readers alive at the end of the first decade of the 21st century the stories seem powerfully resonant, eerily familiar, and deeply troubling. We encounter in this fiction people beat down, distorted, broken, desperate. But we also find characters who are indomitable, resilient, unyielding, determined.

As most good writing, these stories quickly transcend the local and the time-specific.

Any reader, I think, will come away from Tucker's stories with a fully-rounded sense of the diverse characters she has created. Many of them are memorable — a one hundred-year-old waspish woman in a nursing home in "Bless Her Heart," a conflicted schlemiel who unsuccessfully tries to rescue his suffering community from the Depression through his writing, his doctoring, and his preaching in "The Renaissance Man," a young boy who suffers from various deprivations in "Hungers," a grandmother terrorized by her grandson in "A Bunch of Blueness." And the list could go on and on.

Tucker has the requisite skills as a writer not only to pull us into her stories, but to keep our attention throughout. She well understands that authors control the release of intelligence in their stories, often creating small mysteries that have to be resolved by reading further. The story "Hungers," for example, begins with this sentence: "If he hadn't been so hungry, he might never have found out." The use of a pronoun in the opening of a story is frequently used by authors to make the reader search out the antecedent, but to that Tucker adds the mystery of what it is that the "he" finds out.

Flannery O'Connor once said that writers cannot expect readers to see something they haven't first seen clearly themselves, and through her powers of creative imagination Betty Jean Tucker has clearly seen the places, the people, and the things she describes. Her images are often arresting. For example, when describing the violent death of the father of her main character in "When Poets Lie," she writes:

> A big, strong man born to be a logger, Nelson looked away for a second, and a massive pine tree crushed his skull, splaying blood everywhere. Norman could never forget the sticky smears of blood mottled with bark and leaves on his father's face....

In the story "Hungers," another violent image can be seen in this description of the mutilated face of the monsterish Mrs. Landis, who has just been shot: "Her head was no head at all. There was just a big bloody hunk of bone and hair and a few of the little rat-like teeth."

Tucker can describe positive scenes with a similar power.

When the title character in "Callie" first returns from nursing school, she has been transformed. The narrator of the story describes her in this way:

> She wasn't big anymore, and she didn't push her feet along the ground. She walked up the dirt path kinda slow and easy like a lean yellow cat, and she didn't hang her head either. She had on a blue dress and it made the sky around the sun come sliding down, and it looked soft and cool around her....
>
> She come up on the wooden steps, and Grandma said, 'Well, if it ain't the old cow.' Callie kinda smiled a little around the lips, and her eyes stayed blue like the sun shining through water on a knife blade.

Tucker employs similes, such as the one just above, with precision. Describing her younger brother, the narrator of "The Dog That Wasn't A Dog" says "his skin was rich brown like the underside of a magnolia leaf." In "The Taboo Factor," Tucker describes the effects of the Depression on a small town in the Black Belt this way: "The sawmill closed, businesses went bust, and the economic fabric of the townspeople's lives was about as sturdy as cheesecloth." Encountering similes like these, the reader must stand back in awe at how Tucker's imagination works.

One final quality of these stories that strikes me as fine is Tucker's use of what T. S. Eliot called the objective correlative, where the author uses concrete descriptions of place to evoke in the reader a sense of the emotional quality of the scene. In stories that rely so heavily on setting as these, it is not surprising to find numerous examples of passages that create a sense of dread and sadness and a few that create a sense of happiness and hope. Here are two short examples of the former from the opening paragraph of "The Poet's Deer":

> "The Black Belt's July sun is always a prostitute: hot, gaudy, and malignant,"

and

> "A fly hummed across her face, skimmed the corner of her mouth, and made her jarringly awake. She opened her eyes, lay rigid and watched it settle with a tickle on her arm. She slapped viciously at the insect and grimaced when it sailed unhurriedly away. It landed on the window sill and was squatting in the sun leering at her."

The feelings evoked in the reader of these passages do not allow any hope that this will be a happy little tale.

There is much more to say about these stories. I haven't even mentioned the wonderful humor — often grim humor — in some of these stories. I have also not mentioned directly Tucker's masterful use of symbol and her skillful plotting. These and many other triumphs deserve comment. But I do hope that at least this introduction has made readers anxious to take up these stories, and I confidently predict that they will not be disappointed.

Norman McMillan
Montevallo, AL

WHEN POETS LIE

THE first time he saw her, she was a wraith-like presence in the old graveyard of the Make Do farming community. He pulled his wagon load of cotton to a halt in the middle of the drought-hardened dirt road and watched her, a gray ghost moving gracefully among the graves, exploring the history recorded on the tombstones, bending low to read the inscription on a child's marker, caressing with her hand the sharp outline of a tall ostentatious obelisk, then standing still and looking about as if in quest of the answer to old riddles. When she leaned against the trunk of the fabled centuries-old red oak in the center of the cemetery, it was as if the invincible old tree and the dust of the dead both claimed her for their own, and the man in the wagon felt a chill run down his spine.

When she saw him silhouetted against the mid-October sinking sun like some primordial creature, she waved her arm energetically, and he went to her as if summoned to a fateful rendezvous. As he approached her, he took note of the simple gray cotton skirt and blouse and sensible shoes, but it was not until she stepped out from the green aura of the protecting old oak that he got the full impact of the mass of copper curls framing a pale, delicate face. He was stunned by the beauty of the hair, and his fingers, rough and calloused by prickly cotton bolls, itched to caress the silkiness of it. At the same time his head registered regret that the face was a doll's face, too fragile for a farmer's wife during a Depression.

Normally quiet and reserved around strangers, he was emboldened to thrust out his hand and tell her that he was Norman Nelson. She shook it cordially and spoke in such a natural, free way that he forgot his momentary embarrassment over having fastened his overall strap with a nail. She was Cassandra Blankenship, the new teacher whose arrival the community had been eagerly anticipating. She would teach grades one through six in the dilapidated little one-room building that the parents had tried so valiantly to spruce up a bit. She would be boarding with her grandmother, Mrs. Stinson, the postmistress whose store and house were adjacent to the school. When Norman expressed surprise to find her in the graveyard, she gave a little trill of a laugh and declared herself to be seeking her dearly departed vampire family. And the idea of dark vampires and ghouls in the old Make Do cemetery was so funny that he laughed with her and offered to help look, saying that maybe he could find him a girlfriend among them.

They did locate the graves of some of her ancestors and then parted in the haze of approaching dusk as the western sky flamed with watercolor streaks of gold and purple. She had not told him that she was only eighteen years old and had a temporary teaching certificate with only one year of college credits. And he had not told her that he too was eighteen and had decided to return to school. They had sized each other up: She was a professional from the city of Birmingham, and he was a dirt farmer in the Alabama Black Belt. And that made absolutely no difference to either one of them.

When he swung himself up and into the wagon, it was as if his body had been reinvigorated, transformed from the permanent tiredness of body-deforming farm labor into a hopeful strength and dignity that made him square his shoulders and sit soldier-straight on the rickety seat. He slapped the bridle reins on the horses' rumps and directed the drooping horses to "hum up" in a tone of purposeful mastery. The animals responded with a quick start, nostrils flaring, as if sensing a shift in the wind. They must have wondered at the behavior of the man, who suddenly and with great gusto, laughed aloud on the night air. "It's the girl," he could have told them. The girl with copper curls laughing with him in a graveyard at dusk.

Only a mile from home, Norman had just enough time to review his mental calendar of the past four years, in which there had been precious little to laugh about. Memories came spewing into his head in vivid images, lurching from his memory bank in jagged fragments. The Nelson family had endured a psychological tsunami even before the onset of the Depression, with its global misery. The sabotage of dreams for them began with the violent death of Thomas Nelson, which had baptized Norman's mind in the color of blood. A big, strong man born to be a logger, Nelson looked away for a second, and a massive pine tree crushed his skull, splaying blood everywhere. Norman could never forget the sticky smears of blood mottled with bark and leaves on his father's face, the brownish red blood on the ground and Mr. Logan muttering "hell and damnation" over and over.

The calendar slid through the next six months of paralysis spawned by trauma, only to bring more grief when Della Nelson — too fragile and doll-like to pilot the family through an economic crisis — gave up. Making lye soap in the big black pot in the backyard, she succumbed to a stroke, which sent her toppling into the flames of the fire, singeing her tight brown curls. Alive in Norman's memory was the indelible image of Dr. Harrell sitting in a straight-backed chair, blood letting to try and save her, the children watching the flow of blood splattering into the slop jar, with Luke throwing up, and the twins screaming and clinging to each other in the scene of horror.

The sight and smell of blood were thrust upon them again in a sad little tragiccomedy a year later with the accompanying screams of May's frantic wail that Fay was dying, pointing to the blood of menstruation leaking down her leg. And it was blood again when the barefoot Luke, cutting stove wood, almost severed his foot, permanently dyeing the chopping block with crimson. Only Norman had escaped the taint of blood in the Depression saga that had appointed him the patriarch of his truncated family.

And now, shaken anew by the web of red rhetoric staining his memory, he tried resolutely to turn from the morbid musing to more affirming images. But the magic of his encounter with the girl gave way to melancholy, and he vented with a low curse as the wagon jarred over a big rock in front of his house. Darkness closed over his hope for happiness as the night settled into a moonless blackness, leaving him fumbling to unharness and feed the horses, to pour the zinc tub on the back porch full of water for his weekly bath, and to eat the cold buttered cornbread and turnips the girls had left on the stove for him. He lay down on his bed, determined to clear his mind and join his siblings in sleep. But clearing his mind involved a night-long harangue between a down-to-earth Norman, who argued forcefully, logically that he should forget the girl and Norman, the dreamer, who had looked at a girl and dared to dream of the possibility of romantic love. The night blackness pulsed with the passion of his conflict, and finally he gave it up, rising and dressing before time for the cock to crow. By the time the sun was up, he had hitched the horses to the wagon, roused the faithful Luke, and set off for Taylorville to gin his last load of cotton. But he had a plan.

At the gin, where they were the fifth wagon in line, Norman dickered with Tom Parker over the price, both knowing that Tom would give him a better price than usual because he had a soft spot for the Nelson children. Leaving Luke in charge, Norman walked to the courthouse, skirting the row of stores on Main Street with all the wares that he needed but could not buy and finding his way through the old brick building and to the office of the Cahaba County school superintendent. Wade Jernigan was a big man with a big heart, and he swallowed a lump in his throat as he looked over the glasses perched on the tip of his nose at the young man who was the eldest son of his childhood friend. Though he had last seen Norman at Thomas Nelson's funeral, he recognized him immediately, struck by the inroads of the brutalizing effect of poverty in his young face.

Norman, encouraged by a warm reception, quickly delivered his request to be hired as a bus driver for the Make Do School. And to his credit, the school man never mentioned the Depression and the shortage of funds; he just hired him on the spot, and Norman never knew that he was paid from the superintendent's own pocket or that the bus was repaired and maintained through the same source. They went together to the county shop, and Mr. Jernigan gave him the key to the truck and wished him well. Norman was a little disappointed that the bus was really only an old Ford pickup with benches on each side and a tarp for protection from weather.

He did not fully realize the magnitude of what he had done until he drove up to the gin and saw elation brighten Luke's dark brown eyes at sight of the truck. Heart-stopping handsome with a strong, tautly-muscled body, Luke, at sixteen, was a certified dreamer, tragically caught in the overalls of serfdom: bending to the plow, chopping cotton, milking cows, slopping hogs, following Norman without question or complaint, all the while with bitter rue in his heart. The old truck was a tonic, an elixir to break the monotony of the cruel labor that dominated his life. Norman was wise enough to let him drive the truck home, while he himself took the wagon.

On Sunday, he and his siblings donned their church clothes, which the girls had carefully starched and ironed on a padded plank that served as an ironing board. They viewed church attendance as a small price to pay for the joy of a day of rest and sang "Leaning on the Everlasting Arms" without bitterness that the only real arms they had to lean on were their own. They sang "Power in the Blood," and Norman, for the first time since his parents' deaths, thought not of red blood but of the power of a woman's eyes, Cassandra's gem-like blue eyes speckled with hints of green. She was not in church, but Norman's spirits remained high, caught up in the after-church excitement of the children who crowded around him, exhilarated by the prospect of riding to school in the bus and meeting the new teacher. Norman glanced around for Luke and saw him in the center of a group of boisterous boys. It was clear that a baseball game was being planned for the afternoon in George Clem's pasture.

A yearly ritual for the day before school started, the game was more than a footnote to the morning sermon; it was Make Do's own unique bacchanalia, a celebration in hard times of just being alive. The Nelsons arrived early, eager to participate, to validate their existence by laughing, playing, singing, joking, and yelling for the teams in concert with a suffering community, determined to grab happiness wherever they could find it. With people converging from every direction, the twins, pretty and vivacious, ran to the makeshift platform and whipped the crowd into a rousing "Coming Around the Mountain" as Norman and Luke joined in with guitar and fiddle, eliciting a compliment from Maureen Staples, who called, "You do your daddy proud with that fiddle, Luke!"

Norman yelled back, "What about me, Maureen?" And when she teased him with "You ain't no Bill Monroe, Norman. You just keep catching," Norman laughed along with everybody else. He knew he was not a talented musician, but he enjoyed making the sounds of music. Luke, though, was talented, but it was not fame as a violinist that he dreamed of. Nor was it a girl, as in Norman's case. It was the sport of baseball that held his heart, and it was the burning desire to play professional ball and to be recognized by Babe Ruth that kept him alive. Norman knew this better than anyone, and he wanted desperately to give his brother a chance to achieve his dream. Over the years they would practice pitching and catching after a day's work in the fields until it was too dark to see, and they were hungry for baseball news on the radio. Once when Luke was plowing the garden, readying it for planting turnips, Norman left his own work, ran to the garden and took the plow, telling Luke, "Go, go. The Babe is on the radio."

The crowd in Clem's pasture was no less exuberant than a

stadium full in Brooklyn. A call came to clear the field and a rush of little boys fanned out to herd the Black Angus and Jersey cows from the improvised diamond. The music wound down as Red Hankins called out, "We've got a ball game to play here. You Nelsons aiming to play or are you too scared we'll beat you?"

That traditional gauntlet set the game in motion. The Make Dos, with Norman as catcher and Luke as pitcher, took the field against The Others, led by Hankins at the pitching mound. At six feet, six inches tall, with the gaunt, malnourished features common to men in the Depression, he was an absolute terror with a baseball in his hand. Rookie batters who had dared ridicule his cross-eyed visage were brought to their knees in shame at home plate. Every year the game was a duel between Hank and Luke. Norman was the only one who could hit as well as Hank, and Luke, even with his uncanny control and deceptive delivery, was challenged in their rivalry. As a matter of fact, all the players were challenged: they possessed only one ball, which threatened to come apart at the seams; they had only one bat, and the only glove was used by both catchers.

It was no surprise but a source of hilarity that a cowpattie lurking in the grass sabotaged the running game in the third inning when Lance, an awkward first timer, hit a double and slid into second reeking of manure perfume. The fans reacted with wild laughter and colorful, good-natured insults. But after three scoreless innings, they lusted after more dramatic action. When Norman came to bat, the crowd advised and threatened him while he patiently waited for a wicked slider and sent it slamming into the cows' territory for a triumphal home run. He loped around the diamond, ending with a wrestler-size stomp on home plate, where he focused on the prettiest face in the crowd. It was Cassandra, joining in the clapping jubilation of the fans and smiling into his heart. The smile, though, came with only a tentative milligram of hope. The day darkened for him as he realized that she was with Ed Sims and his two little girls.

The gladness of the day echoed in happy guffaws and giggles, in the rustic music of guitars and fiddles and cowbells, in the whacking of bats on balls. But these pleasures receded for Norman, belied the harmony in a tranquil universe which he had previously conjured up. The joy went out of the game for him, but he concentrated ferociously to keep distraction at bay.

Ed Sims. Norman might have expected it. The man had already intruded in Norman's life with a destructive grasp. Now, he lived in comfort in Norman's ancestral home bequeathed to his mother by her forebears in the Bankhead family. Three years ago, when Norman was fifteen years old, parentless and desperate to keep the little Nelson clan from starving, the man, wearing a black suit and hat, strode out of the mist of a November fog onto Norman's porch with a fistful of money and bought the home in a whirlwind of negotiating that baffled the boy, trying to be a man, and left the Nelson children homeless.

The game zipped along, fueled by the crowd's generous rabid support. They pulled for first one side and then the other. When Hankins strode to the pitcher's mound in the fifth inning, cries of "Get 'em, Grim Reaper," hung on the air as Luke scooped up some dirt, dusted it on both hands and clutched the bat. "Strike one," Tom Kent, umpiring, called out, and the hard-bitten Hank settled his face in a fabled frown that darkened his forehead and let fly another strike. "Luke, you a dead man," came a yelled pronouncement from a red-haired nine-year-old who secretly thought Luke was God. Groans went up as the favorite son played Casey at the bat and struck out.

But Norman redeemed the Nelson duo when he scored another home run in the bottom of the eighth and went on a savage streak of aggression in the ninth to throw out The Others' first baseman as he dived clumsily on his belly to try to steal second base. It was The Others' last desperate attempt, and the game was over with Make Do winning by one run. It was amazing, he thought, how winning could make one feel like a conquering gladiator — even without the girl and a lucky talisman.

But the girl was waiting for him as he turned in the glove to Tom Danay and collected his guitar. With Fay and May and a gaggle of teenage girls singing a Grand Ole Opry favorite "Will The Circle Be Unbroken?" Cassandra touched him lightly on his arm, and he turned, knowing it was she. The copper curls were pulled back from her face and fastened with blue combs that matched her remarkable eyes. He imagined his hands on the hair, lying softly on her shoulders, and wondered if the hands that could hold a horse at the plow or slam a ball at ninety-eight miles an hour into a second baseman's fist could ever be gentle enough to trust with such beauty. Suddenly stymied by shyness, he had trouble speaking. She wanted to tell him how much she had enjoyed the game and especially his performance. As she chatted on, he regained enough confidence to introduce her to Luke and the twins. At the gate to the pasture, she did not linger, seeing Ed at his car, waiting for her.

On Monday, Norman awoke with the tantalizing promise of happiness that the dawn seemed to offer, like a chalice of joy, as he readied for the day. It was a day of fragile expectations: he was entering the world of academe, although through the back door; Luke was going to work for FDR's Civilian Conservation Corps; and the girls, who now considered themselves to have come of age, savored the prospect of assuming adult responsibilities on their own.

On this first day, he wanted to make a good impression, so he dressed in clean denim pants and blue plaid cotton shirt and reluctantly pulled on the old brogans, which were in a wretchedly collapsed shape. He fixed himself a lunch sack containing two ham biscuits, located the keys to the bus, and on impulse put into his pocket the nail which had fastened his overall strap last week. He really didn't know why he did that unless it was his rabbit foot. But when he stepped out on the porch, which faced east, a burst of confident optimism swelled within him, and he knew then that he did not need a rabbit's foot. In the full radiance of the sun, now no longer scorching the earth but cascading cool comforting rays across the universe, Norman wanted to salute his world, the land of the free and the home of the brave. He settled for singing, "The skies above are clear again, so let's sing a song of cheer again. Happy days are here again." His route was like a ride into the heart of autumn with the yellows, browns, and shades of red pulsing through the sweet gum trees, dogwoods, and sumac to flow into a picturesque landscape pizzazz.

When he arrived at the school with his volcanic cargo of ten excited aspiring scholars, he experienced a twinge of sadness in remembering the pleasure of his own school days and the gall of having to cut his education short with only a grammar school diploma. His riders piled out of the bus into the school yard, where they joined the Anse boys, who had ridden a horse from their home in what was called Hell's Swamp, three more students who lived near the school and walked, and Ed Sims' two little girls, timid and alienated in their spotless, starched dresses and polished shoes. The presence of shoes on a Make Do pupil was as good as blasphemy, and Jim Anse, his eyebrows arched in indignation, pointed to the shoes, raised his arms in a benedictory gesture, and intoned, "Let us pray."

While Norman was thinking that prayer might not be a bad idea, a sudden hush fell over the group, a sure signal that the teacher was present. Just one look, and Norman knew that they were all smitten. He had thought of her as soft and doll-like. But today, savoring the sight of her in a pale blue voile skirt and blouse with the incredible hair corralled by the blue combs, he felt the strength of her in the high cheekbones, the warm but measured control in her clear distinct voice, the lithe high-breasted, small-waisted body.

"Good morning," she said with a big smile activating a happy dimple. "I'm your teacher. My name is Cassandra Blankenship, but you may call me Miss Cassie. Please remain quiet as you enter the schoolroom." With that, she was definitely in charge and the students trooped into the building. Then, of course, she had to deal with Norman, whose job and presence were a complete surprise to her. He explained his official position as bus driver, but asked that he be allowed to assist her with such practical matters as getting water from Mrs. Stinson's home, keeping the heater going in cold weather, and supervising recess and lunch activities. He made sure that she understood his help would be gratis, that he would be grateful to be in an academic environment, if only in a menial position.

But by the end of that first day, they both knew that they were going to be colleagues, not teacher and janitor. Norman was instrumental in orchestrating the grade levels. He entertained the group of students by telling them Greek myths while Cassandra interviewed each student to gather information about parents, birth dates, health and vaccination issues, and previous education. When she finished, Norman broke off the Orpheus story with a promise to finish it the next day. Then they worked together to move the desks into groups by grade level so that each grade would face a section of blackboards on three walls. The students seemed spurred on by the sense of purpose and charisma generated by their young teachers. With the stage set, the five first-graders positioned themselves facing the blackboard and took up pencils and lined tablets to begin the new adventure of learning by making the first three letters of the alphabet. Norman watched Cassie beam at their clumsy efforts, and he shared her elation.

And it was that kind of feel-good day, where even sad or trivial moments had their own kind of preciousness. Into Norman's memory bank went the fun of showing the students how to fold a sheet of paper to form a cup for the drinking water he hauled from the nearby store, how to hold the chalk for writing on freshly washed blackboards, how to help fourth-grader Bill Anse look up the word "picturesque" and discover with noisy excitement all the things one could learn from a dictionary. There would be sad and funny memories, too, like little insecure Sally Sims crying hot tears onto her tablet because she couldn't make a pretty "A," like Benji, the lone sixth grader, who snickered and rolled his eyes at Miss Cassie's calling Norman "Mr. Nelson," like the expression of sad regret on Cassie's face when Norman told her that the reason all the students seemed older and bigger for the grades they were assigned to was that the school had not operated for two years, and the students had been caught in limbo.

All of the students, except the Sims children, were poor, but they were poorer still because of the gap in their education, and Norman felt that loss and hardship would make most of them well-behaved and appreciative. He could see a serious resolve in their demeanor, a resolve that issued into a fierce determination in the case of Ethel Evans, who ate her baked potato at lunch and clutched her history book possessively. She had a lean and hungry look about her, and Norman knew in his gut she would survive the Depression and succeed. As for himself, he had lived without hope for so long that negativism had claimed his mindset. But today, in an environment away from the heat and dirt of corn and cotton fields, he had been happy and dared to believe in the possibility of a different life.

Loath to leave the day behind, he was glad to linger when Cassie asked to talk to him briefly. She had a surprise for him, she said, and handed him two obviously used sixth grade textbooks, one for English and one for arithmetic. They looked familiar, and he opened them to find his own signature on the title page. His chest hurt with the recollection of his final year in school, a year in which he was on fire to learn everything, to discover the world beyond America's borders, to conquer with Alexander the Great, to solve challenging mathematical problems, to thrill to the rousing ballads of Kipling and Tennyson.

Eagerly, he opened the literature book to page ninety-six, smiled broadly and read with passion and dramatic sweep of his arms, "Half a league, half a league, / Half a league, onward, / All in the valley of death / Rode the six hundred." Inspired by his pleasure, Cassie joined in, and they performed the rest of Tennyson's "Charge of the Light Brigade" with patriotic fervor. They enjoyed the liberating laughter that resulted, and Norman, no longer feeling like a Mr. Nelson, just wanted to touch her. But Cassie was back into her schoolmarm role and led him to a big box of books. "They're yours," she said, unpacking more textbooks for several grade levels and handing him six of his mother's treasured Sir Walter Scott novels.

He was amazed. "Where did you get these?" he asked, brushing dust off *The Bride of Lammermoor*.

"From Mr. Sims. He told me I could have them for the school. He didn't want them."

Running his hand over a handsome leather-bound copy of Bunyan's *Pilgrim's Progress*, Norman could not disguise his happiness. The recovered arsenal of literature brought back the memory of his mother's softly beautiful face bent over a book in the warm glow of a kerosene lamp. How she had loved the darkly brooding Edgar Ravenswood and his fragile Lucy, so tragically driven into madness and murder. Della Nelson had told her children that they could read the novels when they reached their fifteenth birthday. And then she had followed her husband in death, and books had become irrelevant in her children's struggle to survive the Depression.

"When I saw your name in some of these, I wondered how Mr. Sims got them," Cassie said.

Norman tried to speak dispassionately, but it was hard to keep a trace of bitterness from his voice, "When he bought our house and land, he kept everything except our clothes, the radio and our musical instruments." And because he thought his voice would betray him, he changed the subject. "What are you going to do with them?"

"Oh, Norman, you don't understand." Impulsively, she placed her hand on his arm. "I'm not going to do anything with them. They're yours."

"But Sims...."

"Nobody has a right to take anyone's books. That should be an eleventh commandment."

"How about you keep the textbooks for the students who

don't have any and let me take my mother's novels?"

With that, the book matter was settled, but Cassie had another issue on her mind. And when Norman left, he had agreed to teach arithmetic to students in grade three through six. He was going to be a teacher. He could not have been happier if an angel had appeared to him saying, "Behold, I bring you glad tidings of great joy." On the way to his busload of waiting students, he could contain himself no longer and became Charlie Chaplin, exaggerating the famous walk, the clicking heels, the twirling cane as the children shrieked at the fun of their driver. He gave a great whoop, settled into the driver's seat and drove off, singing with the students, "School days, school days, good old golden rule days/ reading and writing and 'rithmetic/ taught to the tune of a hickory stick...." Norman imagined Cassie hearing the echo of the song and joining in. How was he ever going to be with her all day, five days a week and not touch her?

But there was little opportunity to address his personal emotional needs. He met the demands of the teaching role with a religious fervor. He could never have imagined how much pleasure he would experience from learning and empowering others to learn. That pleasure, he knew, was enhanced by the presence of Cassie and her ready acceptance of him in her life. He thrilled at the sound of her voice in the classroom, telling students, "Mr. Nelson will help you with that," "Mr. Nelson, will you help Sissy locate France on the globe?" "We're lucky to have Mr. Nelson." Norman knew himself to be the most fortunate of men, and he ended the first week with a sense of hyperbolic satisfaction.

He and Luke devoted Saturday to tending to the livestock, digging and banking the sweet potatoes, and chopping wood to fuel the stove and fireplace for the winter months. With the languid sun slipping toward setting, he remembered that he needed gas for the bus and hurried to Stinson's Store to fill up. There he found Cassie, tending the store for her grandmother. When she saw him at the gas pump, she smiled and what Norman thought of as her dimple of happiness appeared. When he had finished, she wouldn't let him leave. "Don't go. Come. Sit here," and she patted the porch step she was sitting on.

"Woman," he said, "Don't you know you'll ruin your reputation by sitting with a guy in the moonlight?"

"Sit, Mr. Nelson," she said and he obeyed. "It's dusk and not dark."

"That won't make any difference to people who like to gossip."

"I'm not afraid of them. Are you?"

"Nope. Fact is, I have a reputation for being a stalwart, hard-working man, a mighty fine catch, as the ladies say."

"Are you a good catch?"

"Nope."

"Why not?"

"I'm poor as Job's turkey. I have nothing to offer a girl. The real catch in Make Do is Ed Sims.

"Not for me."

"You're not interested in him? I thought, because you were with him at the ball game…"

"That was because of Grandma. She wants me to be nice to him. I don't know why."

"He's Make Do's mystery man. Just showed up here, the week after the stock market crashed, and made himself at home in my house. Luke and me and the twins were down to zero, scared to death. He had on that black suit and hat, but I thought that money he had was angel dust sent directly from God. He had the money, a legal contract, and an agreement to put us up in a sharecropping arrangement, and we thought we were saved by grace dressed in black. What did I know? I was fifteen and hungry." The memory of the psychic abyss he and his siblings had experienced when the money ran out made him avert his eyes and focus on his limp hands dangling between his legs.

Her voice reached into his pain. Gone was the silky, lilting quality of the laughing Cassie; instead there was the thin, tremulous sound of a little girl. "I know about being hungry, Norman," she said, as the dusk gathered around them.

The pathos in her voice drew him out of his melancholy and back into her world. "For real?" he questioned. "But you lived in Birmingham and went to college...."

"The economy is in shambles everywhere. There were soup kitchens in Birmingham, and people were begging for food. I had to leave college after one year and take care of my dad. He had Black Lung disease, and I..." She paused and then struggled to say, "I watched him die for a long, long year." Her voice broke, and she was just a scared little girl, crying in grief and need for comfort. "One night I got on my knees and begged, begged God to put Dad's pain in my body if only for a little while, so he could rest. And you know what God did? He increased the pain, and Dad was in agony. I wanted to thrust my hands through the skin and muscles of my suffering Dad, down to the bone, and gather up the pain and sling it into the face of God." Her voice had grown strong with fury at the memory, but she was helpless to control the tears washing down her face. Norman broke under her distress. He took her hand, wet from furiously swiping at the tears, and tenderly kissed her palm. When he folded her fingers over the kiss, he could feel her body struggling to regain composure.

They sat in silence until she could continue. "Am I going to hell because I got mad at God?" she asked him.

"If you do, you'll have lots of company — including me."

"It's just that I am an only child and I didn't have anybody to help me. There was so much death, so much suffering."

Still holding her hand, he felt it relax a little. "What about your mom?"

"Another casualty of the Depression. She lost her mind after Dad died. She thought she was starving and hoarded what little food we had. I would find it hidden in dresser drawers, under the mattress, on closet shelves, in shoes — just everywhere. When I cooked and put food before her, she refused to eat, saying that she had to save it for Ben, my dad, who she thought would be coming home soon. She was terrified of thunder and cars and the hoe I used in our little backyard garden. She was sure an evil spirit lived in the hoe and would kill me. In spite of everything I could do, she died, just starved to death."

Because she had shared so much of the intimate hurts of her life, Norman told her about his parents' deaths, and their exchange strengthened them. For a while, they sat, spent, in silence, comfortable in an unspoken commitment. But the sun was absconding with the daylight, and Norman sighed and rose. Looking down at Cassie, he said, "President Roosevelt says things are going to get better. That's what we have to hold on to." And he gave her back her hand, with the fingers still curled tightly over the kiss.

In school the next week, Norman got Cassie to approve of a new unit based on social studies and current events that all students would participate in. With a minimum of disturbance and a maximum of student enthusiasm, Norman created a "play like" version of the presidential fireside chat room. The students bought into his persona of FDR as he sat before them telling them earnestly that he wanted them to understand the world they lived in, and when he launched off into an explanation of government and democracy, even the first graders could understand the basic lesson in civics.

This part of the school day quickly became a favorite time, especially when Norman and Cassie tackled the difficult task of trying to explain the economic breakdown that had brought America to its knees. They admitted that they, along with the best minds in the country, did not fully understand it, but they did the best they could with the rudimentary knowledge they had gained from the radio.

And then, with the dynamic demeanor of an archetypal tent revival preacher, Norman delivered the old cliché of "children are the future" as if he had invented it just for them and urged them to seize the power they possessed to change the world. The little ragtag, barefooted, and often hungry and deprived group were caught up in his rhetoric, ready to go forth and conquer. With the room reverberating with their enthusiasm, he led them into a discussion of what changes they could make in their everyday lives that would help themselves and others be happier.

Suddenly they were all talking. Alicia wanted curlers so she could be as pretty as Verna. Ethel wanted more books; at her house they only had *Grit Magazine*. Jamie longed for a toothbrush. Somebody wished that there was a cure for itch and head lice, and Jim Anse called out, "Don't stop at itch and head lice; what about boils and ringworm?" Evie Mae, a tall, good-looking girl, raised her voice above the hubbub with the plaintive wish that somebody would kill all the tadpoles in her cistern; she had a horror of drinking one from her water bucket. Sadie, a fastidious second grader, pointed out that if everybody had more handkerchiefs, they could stop blowing their noses on their sleeves and spreading cold germs.

Red, with fair skin and signature red hair, wanted something done about the mosquitoes that "eat me up in the summer." Alvin, Luke's admirer, reminded everybody that they needed a ball for play period: "It's important to play some, ain't it, Mr. Nelson?" Benji, usually running his mouth in high gear, had been unusually quiet, so Norman turned to him. "What need do you have, Benji?" He thought that the mischievous child would say something about outhouses and the Sears Roebuck catalog, but he misjudged him. Benji wanted a chair potty for his granny, who was "down in her back" and could not walk. The children became quiet, impressed by the unselfish declaration, and Norman ended the day's lesson with a request that each of the students come up with ideas that might help solve some of the problems they had described.

The next day, students crowded into the room, asking to have the social studies unit first. Verna, still in a glow from being called pretty, tackled the problem of Alicia's straight hair. "Look," she said to her admirer, "you can do it without money for curlers." And she held up her homemade curler, a straight one-third inch wide piece of tin cut from a can and wrapped in paper. "Let me show you," she said, already rolling Alicia's hair on the five "curlers" she had brought. Molly couldn't stand it; she finished rolling the rest of the hair on the strips of rag she had brought for that purpose. With Alicia grinning widely at her beautification process, the class broke into applause. Norman pronounced one problem solved with the community's spirit of make do.

Then came cries of "books, books, books." The little impoverished band had taken Ethel's need to heart and collected a surprising number of books and magazines. Cassie, as elated as Ethel over the treasure, collected the reading material to constitute a lending library that they could all enjoy. There were *Progressive Farmers*, almanacs, one priceless *Saturday Evening Post* with a Norman Rockwell cover, a copy of Mark Twain's *The Prince and the Pauper*, and Augusta Wilson Evans' *St. Elmo*. Everyone agreed that Ethel should have first choice, and she selected *St. Elmo* and dutifully checked it out like a good library patron.

"Now what?" Norman asked expectantly.

Red rushed in with the solution to Jamie's problem. He held up his version of a toothbrush. Benji had to laugh. "Man, that ain't no toothbrush," he declared, but Red was unfazed. "Yeah, it is, you coon. Look," he insisted, holding up a six-inch sweet gum twig with the end split multiple times with a knife. It was indeed a crude brush.

"What you use for toothpaste on that thing?" came the question.

"Soda or salt; everybody's got that."

Norman asked, "Who wants one of Red's brushes?"

When half a dozen hands went up, he asked Red and his cronies to make some more brushes at recess. But Red wasn't ready to leave the stage. "What about my mosquitoes?" he asked.

No one knew how to exterminate mosquitoes, but someone offered that her daddy packed a bucket with rags and made a fire that produced only smoke, which kept the mosquitoes at bay.

Red wasn't satisfied, but he yielded the floor to a little third grade girl who had been waving her hand saying, "me, me, me."

"All right, Rachel. What do you have for us?" Norman encouraged.

"I'm afraid of the tadpoles, too. Afraid I will swallow one from the water bucket and it will change into a frog in my stomach. But I know what you can do," she said confidently.

"What? What?" demanded Evie Mae, who would have broken all the commandments to make tadpoles extinct.

"Take a bucket full of water and strain the water through a thin piece of cloth into another bucket. That way you can catch the tadpoles in the cloth and kill them." It was clear that she would relish the role of executioner.

Norman turned to Alvin and threw him a ball made of twine. "Luke sent us this to use at play period until the economy gets better and we can buy one." Then he and Cassie ended the session with an earnest discussion of health and the regular attention to sanitation necessary to avoid disease and such problems as lice and itch. It had been an exhilarating exercise, and they felt buoyed by the inventiveness and resilience of these children born into undeserved deprivation. They had so much potential that Norman felt confident they would "rise above their raising" and make the world a better place.

For the first time in four years, Norman carried about with him a sense of a purposeful and meaningful life. His spirits were high as he and his siblings participated in the box supper event on Friday night at the school. For this annual fund-raising social, women and girls prepared delicious meals and put them into colorfully decorated shoe boxes. With the identities of the cooks a carefully guarded secret, the men and boys bid on the boxes for the privilege of eating the box supper with the cook. The twins had shamelessly betrayed the code of secrecy and had given hints that would help their boyfriends identify their boxes.

A lot of pretend bribery and speculation heightened the mystery and excitement as everyone milled around the table holding the boxes. Every girl there wanted Luke to buy her box, but no one would give him a clue. By the time Jeb Abrams, the auctioneer, arrived, the crowd was getting restless and reproved him for being tardy. He didn't disappoint them, launching off with a wide crooked smile into a runaway staccato auctioneering spiel. Holding aloft a box decorated with lined tablet paper that featured a crayon drawing of a brown hound dog, he didn't slow down until someone yelled out, "I'll bid ten cents." Actually, given the hard times, that was a good bid, but Jeb scorned it and insisted that the picture of the dog alone was worth more than that. One of the Anse boys won with twenty cents and managed to be gracious when the owner of the box turned out to be Milly Ivers, a good girl who couldn't help looking a little like a cow.

Jeb's energy level accelerated and soon half of the boxes were gone, including those of the twins, who took their dates outside to eat picnic style on a quilt. Without a clue to the identity of the owners of the boxes, but relieved that someone had bought Milly's box, Luke ventured a bid on a box covered in shimmering blue foil and featuring a starched life-like white dove on the top. Norman watched him, proud of his brother's grace and sensitivity, as he took the box and put his hand around the waist of Melany Dupree, a sweet-faced girl made painfully timid by a vivid birthmark on her left cheek.

They went to join the twins outside, and Norman was left, still undecided, trying to guess which box belonged to Cassie. When Jeb picked up a box decorated in red, white, and blue to look like the flag, Norman suddenly remembered seeing some red crepe paper on a desk in the back of the school room. Convinced that the box was Cassie's, he quickly bid twenty-five cents, hoping nobody would bid against him. It was a vain hope. Across the room, with a smug set of his jaw, Ed Sims bid twenty-five dollars. Jeb was rendered momentarily speechless, and a murmur of disbelief went through the crowd. That was the moment when Norman realized with lightning clarity that Sims was his rival. That knowledge did not distress him particularly because he knew that he had youth and personality on his side.

What offended him was the man's gross insensitivity in flaunting his suspect money in a little community as poor as Make Do was.

When Jeb overcame his shock, he looked at Norman. "Can you raise that, Norm?"

"You know I can't, Jeb. I yield to the man with money."

And the auction went on, with Norman betting on another box and sharing it good-naturedly with Widow Perkins, whose jolly manner and homespun yarns kept the young people laughing. Norman refused to think of Cassie with another man, choosing instead to think of what they could do with Sims' money for the school.

But the man was a black intruder into Norman's life and dreams. On the Sunday after the box supper, Sims and his daughters started attending church with Cassie and her grandmother. Dressed in the usual black suit, black string tie, and black wingtip shoes, Sims led his group to an empty pew across the aisle from the Nelsons and arranged the seating so that he sat beside Cassie. Norman knew that some of the ladies thought Sims handsome, with his thick black hair and eyebrows edged with gray, and they were overjoyed at his church attendance, choosing to believe that his sins had been washed away by the blood of Jesus. Men were not so gullible and kept their distance from the dark presence with its dour expression. Nate Huxley remembered only too well finding the Nelson children sleeping on the floor in the empty sharecropper house after Sims manipulated them out of their home.

School days offered no opportunities for Cassie and Norman to have any personal time together, but they managed to have a rendezvous every Saturday afternoon when Norman gassed up the truck. In one of these meetings they had made a pact to help each other in enhancing their education. Norman, who was gifted in the area of mathematics, would help Cassie with teaching strategies for fractions, percentages, and problem-solving, and she would discuss literature with him, using her college textbook. The two young people, sitting side by side on the porch steps and poring over their books every Saturday afternoon, became a commonplace sight, and the community, especially students, knew they were watching something special happening.

But they were puzzled, as was Norman, about the relationship with Sims, who continued to escort Cassie and her grandmother to church. Cassie never mentioned Sims, and Norman was too proud to ask questions. He just determined not to let the man suck the joy from his life and was abetted in that resolve by his immersion in the literature of nineteenth-century England.

Forced into farm labor himself while he was still a child, he discovered Robert Burns, the Scottish plowboy poet, and knew him for a fellow traveler. With a full week of reading and rereading Burns' poetry behind him, he sank down on the steps beside Cassie and said, "I've got a new hero."

"You've given up on FDR?" She was surprised.

"Nope. FDR is still my hero in the political arena. He's going to save this country. But my hero in the literary world is Robert Burns."

"Ah, you've become a Burns devotee. I should have known you would identify with him."

"Well, I do identify with him. His hard life, growing up and scratching a piss-pore living from one hard-scrabble farm to another in the Lowlands of Scotland: that's like my existence here during the Depression. He had farmer's dirt under his nails and an eye for the girls." He cut his eyes at her with a little grin.

"Why else do you like him?"

"He had a passion for the common man and simple life."

"Ah, you've read 'A Man's a Man For All That.' That poem has always been praised for its strong humanitarian views. It's been called 'the Democratic anthem of the world.'"

"When I read it, it gives me goose bumps."

"Did you read 'Holy Willie's Prayer'?"

"I did, but I had a little trouble with the dialect."

"Okay, let's read it and use the footnotes to clear up problems with some of the Scottish words."

With that, and a little preface to define such literary terms as satire and irony and to explain certain elements of Calvinistic dogma, they plunged in and enjoyed Burns' ridicule of cant and hypocrisy in the ribald, earthly depiction of Willie. Then they turned to "Tam O'Shanter," delighting in the rollicking fun of the poem. They grew serious over "To a mouse" and its sobering philosophical conclusion that "The best-laid schemes o'mice and men / Often go astray, / An' leave us naught but grief an' pain, / For promised joy!" Norman refused to linger over the negatives of the human condition and quickly thumbed the pages to love poems.

And before Cassie could clutter his mind with schoolmarm talk about lyricism, rhyming, iambics and pentameters, metaphor and hyperbole, he launched into a reading of "A Red, Red Rose." He was an animated Scotch bard with a Black Belt accent, capturing the power of the impetuous male and his sincere commitment to love.

"Now tell me he doesn't have a song in his heart," he dared her.

"I don't dispute that he's a great lyricist. But in that poem he undercuts the romance by using hyperbole. That's extreme exaggeration."

"Do you mean to tell me that you don't believe the lover will 'love thee still, my dear / Till a' the seas gang dry'?"

"Nope. Absolutely not."

"You don't believe he will love her till 'the rocks melt wi' the sun'?"

"It's just hyperbole, silly."

"You don't believe in everlasting love, Cassandra Blankenship. You are a hard-hearted woman with vinegar in your veins."

He rose and standing before her, he recited the last verse of the poem. He kissed her then. And it was a rose of a kiss—first a bud, then a many-petaled bloom.

Giddy over his boldness, he strode to the truck, repeating

"And I will come again, my luve, / Tho' it were ten thousand mile." Over the noisy motor as he drove off, he heard clearly the sound of her voice calling after him, "I Believe, Mr. Nelson." His smile lit up the truck, defying the darkness with joy.

He shifted the gear into high and sang in a lusty baritone, "Love lifted me; when nothing else could help, love lifted me." He knew that the love in the old hymn referred to the love of God, but it was the love of Cassie that uplifted him, helped him to transcend the disappointments of his life.

He enjoyed the cautious optimism generated by his feeling for Cassie and sought in the poets he admired for evidence that supported his optimism. He found it first in Henley's "Invictus," where the narrator exults: "I am the master of my fate; / I am the Captain of my soul." The words ignited a surge of power within him, a sense of invincibility. He turned to Robert Browning's "Pippa Passes" and was comforted by the poem's conclusion that "God's in His heaven. / All's right with the world." Norman was not a fool: he knew that all was not right with his world, but he trusted the poet, who told him that "Art remains the one way possible / Of speaking the truth...." His excursion into Thomas Hardy's poetry convinced him that Browning was right about art's being synonymous with the truth. This conviction came when he stumbled on the little poem "In Time of 'the Breaking of Nations,'" which expressed an affirmative worldview unusual in Hardy's dark, fatalistic canon. He took his excitement to Cassie.

"You've got to hear this!" he insisted, reading the poem aloud to her. "There," he said, "that says it all."

She was unfamiliar with the poem and asked him what he thought the theme was.

"I think it means that it's the simple things, like a man 'harrowing clods,' or the hearth fires of home, that are meaningful and will last. The story of a maiden and her fellow will not die, though wars and dynasties pass. How does that sound?"

"Sounds like a good interpretation to me."

"It says true. Here we are — you're the maiden, and I'm your fellow, and together we will endure. The poets say so."

His embracement of the affirmative mind-set nourished him like Scripture, and he felt that his life was blessed every time he saw or thought of Cassie.

The golden days lasted until late January. That's when the murmurings, the hushed whispering, the innuendos began to slither through the community like the old enemy from the Garden of Eden. From the beginning of the Depression, Make Do people had bound themselves together in a spirit of genuine compassionate unity that helped them to survive. Nobody wanted it to be true, they shushed each other on the subject, and they prayed for the two young people they loved.

That the two were floundering in a mysterious wasteland was obvious. Before Christmas, Norman had teased Cassie about her disappearing waistline, and she had laughed it off, attributing her weight gain to good country cooking. But by the end of January, it was clear that the extra pounds had settled in her stomach area. She began wearing loose clothes and a big sloppy sweater, which she wouldn't remove, even when the heater was too hot for comfort.

Norman found himself baffled. The twins, hurting for him, recounted snippets of conversation they had overheard. The female population, it seemed, had diagnosed Cassie's condition as a clear case of pregnancy. As extraordinary as it might seem, no one was condemnatory. Cassie had won their hearts, and they were protective of her, dreading what this turn of events would mean for the school and their children.

When Luke heard the talk, he went immediately to Norman, assuming, like everyone else, that Norman was responsible. "I'm not the one," Norman told his brother. "You can't get pregnant with just one kiss."

With the denial, Luke did not question his integrity. "But who could it be?"

They sat for a moment in deep contemplation. Luke broke

the silence. "Could it be that jackal Ed Sims?"

"That's all I can think about. I love her, Luke. And when I think of her yoked to that cold-hearted excuse for a man, I want to puke."

"What does Cassie say about it?"

"Nothing. We don't talk any more. I used spring planting season as my excuse."

"Norm, you got to talk it out with her. You love her, give her a chance to explain."

But a mantle of sadness had settled over him like a shroud, and he hadn't the will to bring up the issue. The days went by with Cassie drifting further and further away from him. With the students, she was still animated and caring, but the laughter had gone out of her voice, and the dimple was no longer in evidence. There was a vague, abstracted air about her eyes, and Norman felt that he was just a zero in her life. But as the end of the spring term neared, he made a trip back to the schoolhouse after taking the students home and asked her to talk to him. She seemed startled and nervous, but she sank into the teacher's chair with a tired sigh.

"We have to have this conversation, don't we?" she asked.

"You know we do, Cassie. It's long overdue."

"I know what people are saying." She tucked a curl behind her ear and leaned forward, eyes unwavering. "But it's not true, Norman. I know I look pregnant but I'm not."

She was so earnest that he wanted to believe her, but cold reason would not accept that. "Everybody thinks I'm the father. Have you told anyone that I am?" When it was out, he cringed at how accusatory it sounded.

"No, of course not. There is no father because I am not pregnant."

"Cassie, be honest with me. There's no use in denying a pregnancy. At the end of the nine months there will be a baby." When she looked away, he pressured her. "Is it Ed Sims? That slime ball from hell? Is that the reason he took his girls and left

Make Do?"

"He left because he heard the talk and thought you were the father. I'm glad he left. Grandma kept urging me to court him because he holds the mortgage on the store."

"When I saw you sitting beside him in church, I wanted to run a sword through his ribs. I'm glad he's gone, too."

"I don't know what to do, Norman. Even my grandma thinks I am pregnant and you are the father."

She was so forlorn he wanted to stroke her hair and hold her hand. But it snaked through his mind that she was probably lying.

"If you are not pregnant, what could be causing the weight gain?"

"I don't know." Her hand went to her stomach, and he read the gesture as a mother's involuntary protection of her baby.

"Maybe you should see a doctor," he suggested lamely, knowing full well that Make Do women didn't consult doctors about pregnancies.

"Grandmama won't hear of it. She's ashamed of my condition, and she's scared."

"Scared of what?"

"We have no money, Norman. I haven't been paid since the first of the year, and when Ed Sims left, he threatened to foreclose on the store."

"But..." he started to protest.

She placed her hand over his and interrupted. "It's not just the money. Don't you see? She's all I have. I can't disrespect and disobey her."

Norman had a sudden thought. "Cassie, did someone rape you? Are you ashamed or afraid to admit it? It's all right. Just tell me what happened."

But she just shook her head. "Nothing happened," she said, seeming to give up on trying to make him believe her.

Norman could detect from her voice and slumped posture that she was in the grip of a melancholy even more severe than his own. But she roused, looked at him intensely, her blue eyes dark with anxiety, and said, "No matter what you believe, I want you to know that I have loved you from that evening when you came to me in the graveyard. I dreamed that we could have a life together, with a house and babies and love 'like a red, red rose.' She paused and then continued as if driven. "But I must tell you this: I'm going to die, Norman." Her voice betrayed no emotion. "I know you may think I'm being melodramatic to play on your sympathy, but I am beyond such conniving tactics. I am even beyond resenting the death of the dream. I will go to my grave loving you, and that is enough."

Her voice trembled then, and the tears came unbidden.

Norman was a strong man's man. But he couldn't bear it. He took her hand, lying open on the desk with fingers curled upward like a beggar's cup, and kissed it. He rushed from the room then, understanding nothing.

He turned to the call of the fields and slavishly followed the almanac in performing the planting, plowing, and hoeing that constitute the farmer's ritual worship of the goddess of fertility. He thought of himself now with an ironic shrug, as the man in Hardy's poem, "only a man harrowing clods," a man brutalized by primitive labor unrelieved by dreams and hope.

He came to know that he had romanticized his life of drudgery by vicarious association with the great plowboy poet. He had been under the influence of the false prophets of poetry. But art and truth, he came to believe, were deceptive, having no more substance than the dust devils floating before his eyes in the blistering air around him.

The implosive relationship with Cassie had left him disillusioned and adrift. Day after day, he followed the plow as if mesmerized, feeling dehumanized and at one with the beast before him. Then it was the middle of June, and on a day pulsating with heat, he was not surprised when a little overalled boy ran toward him as he finished his day's work. "Whoa," he said to the mule and waited for the child to reach him.

The boy was panting. "Miss Cassie's time is come. Mrs. Stinson said to tell you to go quick for the doctor."

"The middle of June," he thought. "Bout nine months." He did not hurry. After all, it was not his baby, though he had once wondered if he could marry Cassie and learn to love the baby. He found the doctor locking his office for the day. "What seems to be the trouble?" he asked Norman, whom he remembered from having attended the young man's parents at their deaths.

"Having a baby," Norman told him.

"That would ordinarily call for a midwife. Why does she need a doctor?"

"I don't know."

"Are you the father?" the old doctor demanded.

"No, sir," he said. Dr. Harrell sighed and climbed into the truck with his black bag. They made the twenty-mile trip in silence. It was dark when they reached the Stinson house, where kerosene lamps lit the hall and Cassie's room. Mrs. Stinson, grim-faced and worried, greeted the doctor and led him to the patient.

Norman settled into a cane-bottomed rocker on the porch, determined to see the strange scenario play itself out. From time to time, screams burdened the air, and in spite of his resolve to be stoic, his body recoiled as if from a blow. He tried to empty his mind of fear, to believe that the human heart can regenerate after all hurts. Suddenly he felt as if his chest had caved in, crushing his heart. He had been a fool. If she would have him, he would love and cherish her and the baby.

By ten o'clock, there were no more screams, no cry of a newborn. The doctor came out and sank down in a rocker as if bone tired.

"Is the baby all right, Dr. Harrell? I didn't hear it cry."

"There is no baby."

"You mean it was stillborn?" Norman asked.

"There was never a baby. She was not pregnant."

"But..."

"When I examined her and found that she was a virgin, I chloroformed her and did surgery. There was something inside of her, all right. An enormous tumor. Dangest thing I ever took out of a human."

Norman felt stripped of his reason. Panic bolted through his chest, and out of the past came Cassie's declaration that she would die.

"Is Cassie dead, Dr. Harrell?" he asked, knowing the answer. Like the Cassandra of Greek mythology, whose accurate predictions were never believed, she had predicted her death and he had not believed her. He had not believed her when she said she was not pregnant. He listened to a mockingbird high in a pecan tree fling a raucous requiem into the still night air. A spasm of despair gripped him and he felt that he had committed the ultimate betrayal. Suddenly, a chilling phrase from the past exploded in his universe of suffering. "Zero at the bone," the old New England spinster poet had written, her mind ablaze with the magic of metaphor. The words lay on his mind like arsenic.

"Yes, Son. There was no way to save her."

And there was no way to save him. They found him in the morning, hanging from a limb of the old oak in the graveyard. Fastened to his shirt with his special nail was a note on lined tablet paper saying, "The poets lied."

THE TABOO FACTOR

MORALITY gets a little muddled sometimes. Take what happened in Milltown during the Depression. The town really wasn't much of a town, but it had a spurt of growth during the twenties — got up to about a thousand population. But then time turned a corner into the thirties into a desperate slide downhill. The sawmill closed, businesses went bust, and the economic fabric of the townspeople's lives was about as sturdy as cheesecloth.

It seemed like the only thing that kept growing was the population. Seemed like the harder times got, the more generous the stork became. It was told that the two midwives had to work in shifts because there were so many babies being born. And that gave rise to the birth of something else — an underground sexual revolution.

It started with a casual comment at the government's work program where the women were making mattresses. Ida Mae, who was blessedly not pregnant, said, "I don't know what Daisy and Rubin were thinking — having another baby smack in the middle of the Depression."

To which the one-hundred-year-old Vera Askew responded with a wicked glint in her old eyes, "They weren't thinking about procreation, Ida; they were thinking about recreation. Sex is the only thing men have for entertainment because it's free."

When the women had laughed in appreciation of Vera's wittiness, a little silence settled over the group, each of whom mulled over her role as sex object entertainer.

Finally, Gloria gave voice to the resentment growing like kudzu in the minds of the others. "I don't know what you all think, but if having fun is what it's all about in these hard times, I don't appreciate it. We're the ones that have the job of rearing the children."

Someone else spoke up in an obvious pique. "It's hardly free. Women pay a high price in the pain of childbirth."

"What's free about the cost of clothes and food for extra mouths?" asked another.

"But what can we do?" The implied defeatist attitude prompted the complaint, "Well, I know one thing. I'm tired of douching and watching the calendar and still getting pregnant."

"Well I'm tired of washing shitty diapers and hanging them on the clothesline to freeze in the winter. Don't misunderstand me now. I love all my five children, but it's all we can do to put food on the table nowadays."

And it was the defining moment for the sisterhood's epiphany: they would just say "no" to their husbands, come hell or high water, and anybody who became pregnant would be an outcast. It was a grave commitment which they knew would require bravery. But as the little network of friends went on a mission to carry the underground message of sexual abstinence, the resolve strengthened, and they championed the cause with a religious fervor.

Of course, they knew at the outset that there were a few women who would not subscribe to the creed because they were too dumb, too cowardly, or too promiscuous. People like Addie Gray, whom they generally tried to excuse on the basis of her having "the can't- help- it's." It was agreed that it was impossible to enlighten some women.

What the conspirators failed to take into account was the power of the male sex drive and the role that the Bottom could play in wrecking their scheme. The Bottom, Milltown's shantytown, sat squatting south of town, with a ditch marking the boundary line between the settlement of mostly blacks and the respectable white community clustered around Main Street. Its houses, all alike except for the degree of dilapidation, hunched on wooden blocks and cast shadows on grassless yards pockmarked with chicken droppings. It sat there, across the gully and out of smelling distance — like a necessary but repugnant outhouse.

Everyone knew what went on there, the blacks who lived there and the whites who visited there at night. The path to Sister Sadie's pleasure palace was well worn, and the Baptists' Women's Missionary Society had crusaded against Milltown's Sodom and Gomorrah for many years. But the Bottom and its illicit pleasures endured, mainly because not even a depression can kill some desires.

It took a while for the women's campaign to make progress, but their sensibleness caused many of the men to recognize their responsibility to sacrifice desire in the effort to survive the bleak hardships of the time. The wives of these men were relieved and relied on kindness and cuisine to keep their mates faithful.

Some husbands, of course, were lost to the Bottom, and in many homes it was a grievous loss. Out of sympathy for the wayward, frustrated men who had turned to Sadie, the town, in recognition of the skewed relations between the sexes, became more tolerant of sin, and the Missionary Society called a ceasefire in their war on fornication. But such tolerance was just a caution light and would not permanently upset the town's collective mindset that miscegenation was taboo for respectable, moral people.

Out of the turbulence and suffering of this time and place grew an unusual love story. It started with Addie Gray, who had been a startling sixteen-year-old beauty, an archetype of the high school beauty queens that smile eternally in the pages of yearbooks everywhere. She had been too pretty and too empty. She read an ad in a romance catalog and, to the consternation of all

Milltown, ordered her a husband, who traveled by bus all the way from California to take her for his bride before the baby came.

She was very proud of herself, for he was a great tall man with strong hands and smiling white teeth, but it didn't take her long to realize that John was a shiftless whiskey addict who made it clear that she was in his life only for his sexual needs. She hated him almost immediately, but for ten years she tolerated his drunken orgies for the sake of their sham marriage.

All the while, she yearned for another man — one that she had spurned at the zenith of her popularity. He was really only half a man, deformed from the thighs down, with feetless dangling stumps for legs. He swung about expertly in crutches, his strong thighs, his hard, broad chest, and the maze of laugh wrinkles on his forehead seeming to chuckle with the capricious nature that had created him. But nature had not been totally cruel. He was a very masculine man. And he was a doctor. That was important, too, for he was a good one to both whites and blacks.

Both men belonged to Addie Gray in a way. John, because she had bought and paid for him, and because she needed a man to make her a woman; Doctor Logan because he was kind and good and surprisingly exciting in a sensual way. And because there had been a time when she had laughed and he had cried and there was a beautiful hurting sadness about the old memory.

For ten years she had shriveled up, inside and out. When she was not bloated with one of her innumerable babies, she was gaunt and flat and wasted. The increasing horde of children pulled at her during the day, and John mauled her tired body in drunken sensuality at night. Then he found a body that was not tired, and he came home late with the stench of liquor and love sweat reeking of the Bottom.

One night he taunted her sadistically, as he stumbled into bed in the early morning hours. "One kiss, my bony sweetheart.

Tonight was a real prize. You know what I mean, Grandma? My love's like a black, black rose. I'm here to tell you that's the sweetest kind of music. Trumpets blare, blare, blaring through the Congo. Boom, boom."

Her silence had irked him, and he had taunted her. "Yeah, and your Doctor Crip was there, too. How about that for kicks? Ain't that a mess now? Ain't it a shame? And him so clean and big shot."

For ten years she produced her babies and accepted the Women's Missionary Society's fruit baskets on special occasions. She was simple; perhaps she did not know that the hurt was only a muted one because Doctor Logan was still free, and as long as this was so, in her heart she thought him hers. Over the years she smiled less and fertilized the bitterness in her heart.

At last the Depression waned and Addie Gray collected checks from FDR's welfare program. The lean thirties became the forties, the old moral codes reasserted themselves, and fornication was no longer acceptable. And suddenly the other woman was there. She was a very young woman, the new public health nurse. She brought with her a softness, a cleanness, a young Holy Grail kind of excitement that made those near her smile and walk a little taller. She came from Saint Vincent's Hospital in Birmingham, from its antiseptic smelling corridors, from diet-right food trays, from oxygen tents and chrysanthemum-scented bedside tables to the land of the snotty-nosed Negro urchin and the welfare clientele. Here she had to pass another kind of examination, the kind that only the Bottom can create.

Her name was Helen, and she was a tall girl with shiny straight black hair and a bewitching smile. Her father, an English professor, had said, "We're academic people, Helen. Nursing is for women with strong stomachs." Her mother, diminutive and nervous, agitated her tea and pleaded, "Don't go, Helen. All those Negro shacks like in Lillian Smith's books. You know you couldn't bear it."

But she did bear it. Every morning she got up early, walked out on the porch of her boarding house, stretched out her arms and looked at the world and found it to be good. She smiled at the goodness and it smiled back at her, and at first the Bottom was only the place where there was so much squalor and disease. And she did not listen, really listen, to the insinuations about what went on in the Bottom. She breezed along the country roads from clinic to clinic, rubbed alcohol swabs over dirty skin, accepted the gratitude, loved life, and left the genuineness of her charisma lingering after her. She had no problems, many friends, and was not plagued with complex desires concerning men. Her life and needs were simple.

Then the day came when she realized, with a shock, that Doctor Logan was a man. Not just the county health doctor, and not just a cripple, but a male with a male body and very male inclinations. And from that day, life was no longer simple.

It happened on clinic day at a rural community south of the town. The last patient had gone, and they were going to ride back to town together in Doctor Logan's car. He hoisted himself up expertly under the steering wheel, posing his crooked leg stumps above the specially rigged brake and clutch system. Helen's door would not close securely.

"Well, damn it to hell," she said in a soft explosion of tired exasperation.

The doctor threw back his head and laughed, the lines in his forehead wrinkling in merriment. She relaxed in the sound of his laughter.

"I'll get it," he said, twisting his body quickly and unselfconsciously along the seat toward her. Steadying his right arm on the car seat behind her, he reached his other arm across her, accidently brushing her breast. With a powerful grip he jerked the door into a secure position and locked it.

He was so close to her, and all she could think of was the terrible masculinity of the thick black hairs covering his arms and showing at the open neck of his shirt. His breath stirred her hair.

She stared at the triangular patch of curly dark hair at his shirt opening and couldn't lift her eyes to his face.

"Look at me," he commanded, his voice soft but forceful.

"I can't," she said, but her eyes moved upward to his lips.

"The hell you can't." He was almost whispering. "We've been going around here not looking at each other. Now that's got to stop. I want you to look me in the eyes and see that I'm a man. Forget about the legs. Tell me what color my eyes are."

Still she couldn't look up. "They're blue,' she said, "cold blue. I don't like your eyes."

"Do you like anything about me?" She sensed him tense. Suddenly, she couldn't stand it. She took his face in her hands and traced the outline of his lips with her finger. "I like your mouth," she said.

It could have happened then, but it didn't, for they were afraid of themselves. But a beautiful, painful ecstatic need had been born, and they hugged it close to themselves, bewildered and tormented and happy. So they drove home in silence.

And the silence lasted a long time. No words came to stir the stillness of their peculiar maelstrom. It was a waiting time, when both strained and listened for words that would not come. An infinite space, where no wind blew and no flowers bloomed, seemed to push them further apart. They worked together, their hands tremulous and their eyes averted, and they talked over the phone in serious, cool voices about arrangements to send a polio patient to Birmingham, or about death certificates, or about anything else that did not really matter. And in the nights, each would lie in his bed and imagine himself close to the other.

Then into the silence of the days and nights slithered more

suggestion of the sickening Bottom-like stink that tantalizes the minds of neurotics and diseases the pure in heart. It came in little drifts. Scraps of overheard conversation challenged Helen's smile. Miss Winters rocked on the darkened porch of the boarding house and told her companion, "I never did believe that story about Emmett Logan, but still it would be a shame for that nice girl…"

And the Negro woman who ironed her uniforms looked at the troubled young woman and said, "He's been mighty good to us colored folks, Miss Helen. He comes ever time somebody bees sick, and he comes even if'n you can't pay. He's just a good man, any way you look at it."

And still the words were all about them and not between them. They spoke only in those cool, serious nurse-doctor voices in the shade of the shadow. They waited for the shadow and the silence to move, to make a sign but it didn't happen.

And all the time Addie Gray was there, watching and waiting and dying a little from the cancerous knowledge that ten years and a young girl had finally made malignant. At the maternity clinics which she frequented because another baby was on its way, she saw the deliberately untouching hands, the coolness that was love. She became Eve and Jezebel and Lot's wife, and she knew what she had to do.

She went to the clinic on a day when she knew the doctor was not scheduled to be there. Her baby was expected in two months.

Wrapping the blood pressure apparatus around her arm, Helen thought how much Addie Gray looked like a hollow skeleton in an abstract painting.

Addie Gray was too casual. "How long you known Dr. Logan, Miss Burke?"

"Well, I didn't know him until I came here about eight months ago."

"You can't learn very much about a man in eight months, can you?"

"Oh, I think you can learn the important things, don't you?" Helen was wary.

"Depends on what you think is important, I guess. What do you know about the little doctor?"

Helen hated the woman, but she knew that she could not show it. "I know he's kind and compassionate and one of the best doctors I've ever known." She recorded the reading on Addie Gray's card. "His professional accomplishments are remarkable, everything considered."

Addie Gray grabbed at the phrase. "Yeah, 'everything considered' is right. Him being a cripple, everybody thinks it's so hot when he ups and becomes a doctor. There's even folks that look over all sorts of things just because he's a cripple." Her bitterness reverberated in the room. "I could tell you a few things about Dr. Logan. Him and me grew up together. Our folks worked tenant farms right next to each other on the old Haskins Place, and when old man Haskins died, he left Emmett enough money to go to medical school. He always did think Emmett was something, from the first time he seen him hit a baseball and scramble around the bases on his stick crutches. Emmett, he used to be sweet on me. Didn't know that, did you? I was a looker then. Coulda had just about anybody I wanted. But I wasn't about to tie myself down to a cripple and feel them stumps of legs in the bed with me. No, sir. I got me a real man."

Helen felt embarrassed to look at her. "Well, I only know him in a professional way, of course, but I respect him highly." There was too much dignity and aloofness in her manner. It pricked Addie Gray.

"Oh, come on now. You know you been thinking things 'bout him. Everybody knows it. That's why I'm gonna tell you something. I figger I owe it to you, you being new here and young, en all. Now don't let it throw you, but our Doctor Logan's got a little side practice over in the Bottom. Makes you feel funny, don't it? When I think of him and me when we were growing up..."

Helen shut her mind to the words. The shadow was all about her, and her own words sounded as if they came from a deep abyss. "I don't like that kind of talk. Now, I've got to get my needles sterilized. The waiting room is full of patients." Her hands became busy, and she moved jerkily.

Addie Gray got ready to leave. "You don't need to say nothin' about whut I just said. Remember I told you though." And she was gone.

High screams penetrated the diseased hollowness she left behind as a towering pregnant Negro woman lurched into the room with her three-year-old son in her arms. The child writhed in pain.

"Oh, Ella, you've let his hernia get strangulated!" Helen's numbness vanished as she hurried to take the suffering child. She had repeatedly urged the woman to have the boy cared for before this happened.

"I'se don't know whut it is, Miz Helen, but he's yelling like dis ever since five o'clock dis morning. De rupture done come down on him, and I can't git it back like you showed me. Hit got stuck afore, and we got it put back, but dis time it just wouldn't go."

Helen laid the child on the treatment table and pulled his trousers down. She touched his body gingerly, and the boy twisted in pain. His screams were terrible.

Taking his temperature rectally, she thought about the possibility of gangrene. If the hernia had been strangulated since five o'clock, it would be only a matter of time before the poison set in. "You'd better run across the street and ask Dr. Logan to come help me, Ella," she directed.

Alone, holding the tortured child down on the table, Helen

was suddenly nauseated. She looked at the form on the table, and it blurred to become a strange half-man, half-boy image with laugh wrinkles in the forehead and sensitive lips that twisted in derision. The vision was gone quickly, but it left her shaken. She gripped the boy's arm more tightly, not caring that she was hurting him.

She could hear the doctor's scrunch-thump approach through the outer office as the rubber tips of his crutches signaled every step. His pleasant greeting to the waiting patients and their respectful replies eased her anguish. He was the doctor, and he would take care of everything.

"Good morning." He spoke to her casually and went directly to the child. Helen pulled his stool up to the table and took his crutches. He examined the child skillfully.

"It's going to take something drastic to reduce it. What's his temperature?"

"One hundred. And he's probably been ruptured since five this morning."

"He'll have to go to Lamon for surgery before gangrene starts." He looked at her for the first time. "How do you feel, nurse?"

"Fine," she assured him.

"We'll have to put him to sleep. You realize that, don't you?"

"Yes." She began preparations to administer the seconal. And all the while she felt as if she were outside herself, looking down from a great distance at a terrible monstrosity. She reached into the doctor's bag for the needle, still in that soundless, motionless trance where the mind is apart from the body and goes madly into doubt and despair. She was caught up in a whirlwind of searing images and hypnotizing refrains that electrified her psyche. With arms thrown over her eyes, the trance took her through the door of the Bottom, where pale pygmies and Amazon Negresses gyrated to the savage sorcery of voodoo. The pagan sounds of a primitive night screamed and pounded around her, a throbbing drumbeat pounding out a little side practice in the Bottom, a side practice, side practice. The whirlwind would not stop. It sped on and on, propelling her from one distorted mirror to another: a strong white hand on a voluptuous black breast, white lips on a black baby, a black hound snarling in the death throes. All with the drums beating out their side practice, side practice, while little white flutes insisted a good man, any way you look at it. The momentum stopped still before a painting of a stiff white gargoyle with black hair over its eyes and a maniacal grin across the face. The gargoyle sat hunched forward before a deep black ditch from which grew black trees that reached to black skies. Then the drums went into slow motion with a now muted chorus of side practice, side practice, a little practice on the side. And the dueling flutes, gathering strength, sang out hosannas for the good man, the man who is good no matter how you look at it. Caught up in the triumphal sound of the flutes, she succumbed to awe, and the whirlwind was gone.

Her arm was hurting. Her trance surrendered to Dr. Logan, who relaxed his grip on her arm and took the needle from her, slowly easing it from the boy's arm. "You've given him too much. How many cc's did you use?" His eyes were bright and his voice quick.

She looked at the tourniquet on the baby's arm and at the death-like stillness of his body. "I don't know. I can't remember." Her fear was acute.

The doctor's hand did not hesitate over the hernia. The lump moved and obeyed his hands. "Do you remember tying the tourniquet and inserting the needle in the child's arm?"

"Oh, God."

"Tell Ella to get her brother here quickly to take this baby to the hospital. He'll be all right, but we need to get him on to Lamon today while he's still asleep."

"Oh, God."

"Shut up and do as I tell you, nurse." His voice was hard but not unkind. "When you've told her, go to the rest room and wash your face and hands."

When she came back, the patient was gone, and he was checking the first of the maternity cases.

"Did you wash up?" He asked.

"Yes, I'm clean now. In fact, I feel purged."

It was a long afternoon, but they finished it in tired peace. Afterwards, sitting across the room from each other, enjoying their cigarettes, the shadow moved and the silence spoke.

"You could have killed him, you know."

"Yes, I know. I could have killed you and myself, but I didn't."

"Have you come to terms with it?"

"With what?"

"Whatever you were wrestling with."

"Oh, that." And she did not know where to go from there.

"Was Addie Gray here today?" His intuition was uncanny, she thought.

"Yes."

"Did she tell you the story she has spread that I have a practice on the side in the Bottom?"

"Yes."

"Did you believe her?"

"No. It was only a shadow problem."

"Gave you a moment's pause, though, didn't it?"

"Only a little."

"Good. Addie Gray's myth derived from the time her mail-order husband saw me in the Bottom one night. He was doing his thing at Sister Sadie's, and I was delivering a breech baby a block away."

"I don't need an explanation."

"Well, I need you to know the truth." He took a long pull on his cigarette and ground it out in an ashtray. "I don't want the taboo factor to mess up our relationship."

"And what exactly is this relationship we have?"

"I thought you knew. It'll be a husband/wife relationship. Nothing taboo." He held her gaze steady and delievered his own version of the classic proposal. "I love you, woman. Now come here and say you'll marry me."

And she went, like a homing pigeon, hearthappy that there was no taboo against loving a legless man.

The Dog That Wasn't a Dog

BEFORE the dog came, when I was fourteen, I needed no one. There was just Joe and me, growing up together in the old Smith house just outside the city limits.

We got along all right, Joe and me. We didn't know any better than to be alone, ever since that morning I woke up and She was gone. I remember the welfare lady had a word for it — "desertion." I didn't know what it meant then, but it didn't matter much, except that Joe was so little he didn't know better than to love Her. I didn't know much, so I let him cry at first, but I learned and we got along all right by ourselves, Depression or no Depression.

I didn't even need Joe. I could have got along all right without him. Even better, maybe. He was just a little boy, always in the way when I was at Mrs. Kinnard's cleaning or at the café washing dishes. But when they came to get him, after She left, he cried and begged, "Neldy, Neldy, my Neldy." And they didn't take him after all. I don't know why they didn't unless it was just hot and the woman in her white starched dress didn't want to get mussed from him being dirty and crying. Sometimes now I wish they had taken him on then. I didn't need him no more than I needed Her, and maybe I would not have got so mixed up after the dog came.

But he stayed with me, and I got him clothes, fixed toys for him, and washed him. I never did really touch him, though, and soon he understood the not-touching. He was so pretty and soft, sometimes it made me want to cry, but I couldn't kiss him and hug on him like some folks would've. From the very first, I meant for him not to love me. I weaned him to need nobody, like I weaned myself, and that's the way I knew it had to be.

That's the way it was before the dog. As Joe grew up, I liked him for the part of him that was like me, and I was proud of him. We lived by ourselves, alone together and yet apart.

You didn't see that part of us that was alike when you looked at us. I was skinny with splotched skin and stiff, smutty-looking hair, and I had purplish eye pouches that made me look like an old woman. It seems to me that I must have been born with sores on my legs because even after the time when other girls — the clean, soft, giggling girls with nickels for recess — were shaving their legs, I was picking scabs off boils. I was so ugly I didn't even like myself. I cringed before the beauty of pretty faces and white hands twined together, swinging down the street in laughing, whispering intimacy. The sweet deliciousness of shared secrets was never mine, and I wouldn't let myself hunger for it. I didn't really need it anyway. No more than I needed Her or Joe.

It wasn't hard for me to be unloved or for people to leave me alone, but with Joe it was different. He was beautiful, with a man and little boy and womanness all mixed up in a way that made people want to touch him. Only they never did, because he was like me in that special way. I watched him grow up, and always the smooth darkness of him hurt me. All of him was dark. His silky, straight hair was night black, and his skin was rich brown like the underside of a magnolia leaf. Sometimes at night, after he was asleep and could not know, I would reach out and stroke the soft, warm skin of his back. I didn't do it often because it made me sad and hollow inside.

After She left, I taught Joe to be a man before he was a boy, taught him to live without before he lived with, and he almost learned.

It was like the time they pushed him in the town water trough when we were coming home from school. I don't remember what the fuss was about. The reason didn't matter anyway. The thing was that I had always wanted to see somebody in that trough. I was glad in a way it was Joe because he was beautiful, and the thing was nasty, and I guess I might have thought it would make him ugly. I don't know why I could have wanted that, but I might have. It was a gray oblong stone trough across from the jail and the bottom and sides were lined with a green slime, the water gurgling with rotted stuff. They threw him in and smeared his face with the slime, and I watched.

When they turned him loose, he stood up in the trough, his clothes dripping darkly, and flung his wet hair back from his face. Without taking his eyes off the boys, he wiped his face with his shirttail, and his mouth didn't move and his eyes didn't cry. So it became unfunny and they went away. I was the only one who ever saw Joe cry, but that was after the dog came.

The evening of the water trough, we went home together, and he said why didn't you help me. You can take care of yourself, I said, not wanting him to know I knew he didn't want any help. I'd a kilt you if you'd said anything, he said, and I was proud of him. We went on home, liking each other.

But that was the last time like that. Because the dog came, and the first time I saw it I kicked it. I don't know why, or even whether or not I meant to. Maybe it was because she was dirty and pregnant, and you could see the fleas running in and out of the greasy-looking brown and white spots. Maybe it wasn't that at all, but rather that she was like somebody, like us or like Her. That first time, I was sorry. Not for the dog. I didn't care that she was hurt. I don't know, but I think I was sorry.

It wasn't right that the dog's eyes should be so like Joe's, so large and richly dark. Maybe that's why he wanted her. Because he saw the eyes when he bent over to feel her brittle ribs where I had kicked. And then the dog twisted her heavy body around and licked his hand. I remember thinking then, standing in the kitchen door watching them, that it would be all right. I could feel Joe shiver, knowing it made his flesh creep to be touched. He sat down on the porch step and looked at the dog. She didn't approach or tuck her tail and slink away. Just faced him, admitting a mistake and promising that it wouldn't happen again. I was ashamed for watching them watch each other. So I was glad the night was coming in fast and the dog would go away.

That was in the transition to darkness when it's hard to tell light from dark. That was when I thought the dog was a dog.

But it didn't go away. It was there all the time, growing bigger and bigger and making a fool of me. I hated it for being a mama dog, and I hated Joe for being the way I wanted him not to be, for having a stupid heart, a little boy heart that let a dog slobber on it.

At first, Joe was ashamed before me about the dog. We can't let the mutt starve, he'd say, with his dark, soft eyes looking past me. And I wouldn't say anything. I never did say anything, but he knew. He knew something else too, something about the dog that I should have known.

He learned everything about her in the few weeks before she got sick. He knew her better even than he knew himself, or me, and he talked to her with silly love when he thought I could not hear. She would stretch out at his feet in the dust with her tongue panting from the heat, and he would sit for hours talking low to her and picking and killing ticks and fleas.

One time he almost got killed for her. He acted that way about her, like she was Jesus Christ or something. It was when Mr. Reen caught her sucking the eggs in his hen house. She'd been doing it a long time, he said, and so he got his shotgun and waited for her one evening. It was about the time Joe was coming along the road from school, and when he heard the first shot, he began to run without knowing what it was about, and yet in that funny way seeming to know too. When he saw the dog come limping and howling out of the chicken house, he ran for her like mad and grabbed her. He was holding her, and both of them were yelling and wailing with the dog bleeding all over him. It happened so quickly, Mr. Reen couldn't stop his shooting, but the shot missed them. The old man had a heart attack from coming so close to killing Joe, and when he got over it and Joe went to see him about working after school to make up for the eggs his dog destroyed, Mr. Reen wouldn't hear to it. Said he had already been paid in full. We didn't know what he meant by that. It didn't matter anyway. He was old and sick, and I knew he had not learned much in his life.

Then the dog was sick, a gut-splitting sick, for three days, and the burlap sack bed under the house smelled of greasy shed hair and vomit. Every time Joe crawled to her, I told myself thank God she will die and he will be the same again. He crawled in and out, in and out, and the third night he slept all night with her. When he came out, I saw the saliva wet on the blackness of his hair, and I shivered.

That was the day he had to cut grass for the Fentons. I ought not to leave her, he said, but he didn't look at me, and I knew he would go. He got ready, slow-like, and went again to look at her. Come here a minute, he said, and I went and squatted and looked at the dog. She's trying to have her pups, ain't she, he asked, like he knew already, but wanted me to say it. Yeah, I said, squatting and watching. She was stretched out, her head limp on the ground and the specks in her eyes mingling muddily. Her bones stuck out, and her shriveled tits were sucked up into the big bloated belly that jerked and strained. She didn't see us, but her blue-streaked tongue gave a tired lick when Joe put his hand on her head. Something's wrong, I know, he said then. Let's get the vet. Something's wrong. I knew something was wrong, but I didn't let on. What do you know about having puppies, I said. They all act like that. Go on now.

I got up and went into the kitchen hearing him call all right now. I'll work and pay him for it. I think you better do it now.

When he was out of sight, I went back to the edge of the house and watched. She was whimpering then, and the side of her mouth on the ground was caked with dirt. For a long time I watched her — her with a belly full of life that never would be life. When the blood started out of her mouth and the birth hole, I said bitch, bitch, bitch, until she looked at me and saw me saying it. It wasn't long until her sides were still and the gray ground was dark purple, and I was glad, only I didn't feel good because she had seen me, and I wished she hadn't.

I stayed squatted down there a long time in the hot, white death air and the gladness oozed out of me, so I could smell myself sweat. I went inside and it was even hotter. I couldn't breathe, and finally I vomited. I didn't like myself then, and I shook to think of the dead thing under the house. I shook, and I thought of Joe and the dog that was something other than a dog and I was afraid.

I felt him coming home fast and knew that his dark, pretty eyes would be old with his worrying. I saw him stoop down to look under the house, and then nothing showed but his hands — long, strong, clean hands holding to the floor. At first they were very still, like held breath in a spasm of fear; then they jerked and scratched the plank so that the gray porch splinters stuck under his fingernails and made the blood ease out. And still his hands scratched. Then they dropped to the ground, and he rocked and moaned hurting moans with the flies swarming around, and the ants crawling greedily.

I wanted to hold him like when he was a baby and blow the silky blackness away from his forehead, but I couldn't, and it hurt so bad. I couldn't because I felt dirty and ugly, like sin. It was the dog, that dirty bitch of a dog.

Suddenly, the heat exploded in a dry, crying gust of wind. The bright whiteness of the sun died like an electric light turned off, and the daylight was dark. Joe staggered from under the house, his little boy arms filled with the dog and her sagging load. He was crying, and when he laid his head against the dog's, a big blotch of blood from her mouth smeared across his face. He put her down just a little way from the house and got a pick. He dug her grave, propelled by silent, jerking sobs, while the streaked lightning made his hair blue-white, and the wind hurled the dirt back into his face.

The rain waited for him. When he was through with the

mound, and the cross was in place, it came plunging down, slicing through the heavy air. Then he was at the bottom of the high porch steps, looking at me. He looked, and he was not crying anymore, and his soft eyes were not soft. Then he was like me, like me the morning I woke up and She was gone. He was like me then, and I thought thank God, it's over and he'll be the same again. He didn't really need the dog.

But then I could see the storm in him, and when he started talking, it was like the thunder was churning up his insides. You killed my dog. You killed her just the same as you'd picked up the ax and hit her in the head. I knowed you wouldn't get the doctor. I knowed it.

He started walking fast toward the road. Once he looked back and then started running like he was racing with the hot rain. He became legs, shining legs, then nothing.

It's been a long time now. I can remember him running, running away in the rain, and my heart runs after him sometimes, but he is always ahead of me. Sometimes I can feel that I'll catch him because I almost know what it was about the dog. But then it eludes me — that thing that Joe knew and I didn't — and I can't remember anything except that before the dog came I needed no one. But the dog did come — that dirty bitch that wasn't a dog.

A Bunch of Blueness

ALL of her life she had fled from the pain of the past and yearned for the rainbow in her future. As the years went by, her husband died of a heart attack, her daughter deserted her for the streets of Chicago, and the days crawled by, empty and joyless.

But on Mother's Day one year, a telegram came, and she was dizzy at the prospect of having a child, her grandson, come into her life. A loving relationship with him would fill a void and make the little Victorian cottage echo with laughter. She would bake chocolate chip cookies, buy Spray and Wash to remove grass stains from his tee shirts, and stock the medicine cabinet with Band-Aids and cough drops. And she would have to remember to put her dentures out of sight at night, to make rules about wiping one's feet on the doormat, to be sweet to his friends, to get him a set of World Book Encyclopedias. And, of course, she would write to Lucy Baxley, Alabama's treasurer, for membership in the state's Prepaid College Tuition Plan. She was giddy over finally capturing the elusive future and the happiness it promised.

But moving the future into the present is a tricky business, she discovered. The vision of rainbows evaporated as the twelve-year-old boy stepped off the bus. The epitome of the dirty, ragged street urchins she had seen on television, he looked sullen and defiant, a barely suppressed anger lurking in cold gray eyes. He was burly for a twelve-year-old, with the craggy look of a Nordic Abraham Lincoln. "So blonde," she thought, "not at all like my people." It was hard to believe he came from her daughter, with her sweetness and dark features.

"Craig?" she asked tentatively.

"Yeah," he finally admitted, looking somewhere to the left of her.

"I'm your grandma, and I'm so glad you've come to live with me." She tried to sound sincere and suppress her dismay.

"Well, I ain't staying long — just till Mama gets well," he informed her, shifting his duffel bag to his right hand.

But he stayed. She had had eager hopes that he would be her salvation. Now, four years later, she felt damned. Consumed by God-knows-what resentments of his previous life or of the grandmother whose age and lifestyle baffled him, he dropped out of school on his sixteenth birthday and allied himself with a group of redneck scum in a nearby Alabama Black Belt town.

For her part, she resented the pollution of her life by someone so worthless, resented the endless calls from the police, the refusal to work, the squalor of his room, and the thumping rap music that sounded obscene, careening off walls covered with wallpaper featuring pretty pink cabbage roses.

He pleasured in heeping indignities and cruelties on her, and she grew increasingly intimidated. For years he had responded to every correction or reprimand with an explosion of anger. Often she was inert with fear, especially after that terrible confrontation about a car.

"I'm old enough to have a car now," he had informed her between slurps of Rice Krispies one morning.

She was caught off guard. "Well, are you old enough to pay for it?" she asked, unable to conceal her indignation.

"What the hell you mean by that?" His voice crawled with antagonism.

"I mean that since you've quit school, you should get a job and work to buy yourself a car. If you saved half of each paycheck, you could have enough in a year to make a down payment. Why don't you call Skeeter Jones down at the tire place? He would be glad to help you."

"I'll be damned if I ask one of your do-good buddies for anything. You want me to ask him to pray for me to get a car? I'll just do that and wait for a Camry to drop down in the front yard. I just bet there will be a note on it that says, 'In God We Trust'."

Not stopping to consider consequences, she pointed an accusing finger at him. "One day God will strike you dead for such disrespect."

He hurled his bowl across the room, shattering the window above the sink. "It ain't God that's gonna strike you dead old woman," he promised, wiping the milk from his mouth with the back of his hand.

She did not buy him a car. What she did was have a lock installed on her bedroom door, and she was never again without fear in her own house. In her life she had endured great hardships but never had she been the object of such hatred. She censored everything she said and tried not to provoke him. She endured daily verbal abuse and lost her self-respect because she dared not assert herself to change the situation.

The temptation of suicide snaked itself into her consciousness, and she began to wonder how many of her anti-depressant pills it would take to kill herself. She had once seen a movie in which a cancer patient had taken ten Melaril tablets, and it was enough. But she didn't know what milligram the pills had been. Hers were only .25mg, and she thought ten might not be enough. She dreamed of botching the attempt and living paralyzed and helpless, with her grandson wiping out her little savings and tormenting her with temper tantrums and threats.

His malevolence manifested itself in assorted cruel acts. Once a neighbor had delighted her with a gift of garden vegetables, and the purple hull peas reminded her of those her husband had grown when they were first married. In spite of the arthritic crippling of her hands, she set about shelling the peas in eager anticipation of the meal she would prepare. From the past came a recollection of opening the hulls, running her thumb down the row of peas to plunk them into a pan, always alert in case a worm lurked inside the hull. She could close her eyes and see the black pot on the old iron stove, its contents of peas, water and a thick slice of fatback sending forth a hunger-inducing aroma. How swift her fingers had been then. Now she endured grotesque pain, relying on her thumbs and one index finger to gingerly remove the peas one at a time. It took her three hours, and she was aware that her grandson watched her covertly while pretending to be absorbed in a television program.

Hoping to engage his interest, she said, "I'll bet you've never shelled peas have you?"

"Don't talk crazy. What would I be doing shelling peas?"

"In my day, everybody shelled peas when it came canning time."

"That ain't nothing to me."

"In the Depression, everybody worked if they wanted to eat. Nobody thought he was too good to work."

She knew she should hush, but it was galling to have to bite her tongue in fear of an obnoxious threatening teenager. She held her swollen, purple-stained hands in front of her and watched them tremble in terrible pain.

"Well, in my day, only stupid people work. Picking peas out of a hull one at a time. What kind of work is that?"

"It's work that puts food on the table, that's what. Mr. Trager, your grandfather, always loved purple hull peas, and I do too."

She was not prepared for his reaction. He leaped from his chair and strode to her, cheeks flaming. He leaned down, his face so close she could smell the sourness of his breath, and she noticed that he would be shaving soon.

"Well, let me give you some more work to do. You're gonna love this, grandma." His mouth curled into the habitual sneer he had perfected. Taking the pan from her loose hands, he opened the back door and hurled the precious peas in a wide arc over the yard. They glistened in the hot July sun, hovering, then falling in seemingly slow motion into the grass and sand.

On the television, a vinegar-voiced talk show host prattled about Jenna and Barbara Bush's attempt to buy liquor with a fake I.D. "They should be held to a higher standard because they're children of the President," shrilled an indignant guest, spittle erupting as she spoke. "It's just liquor and a lie," Estelle wanted to say. "It's not evil. I know evil. It is here with me, walking toward me, grinning, putting the pan so gently in my lap, patting my hand saying, 'There, there, Grandma.'"

She knew evil, and she knew that it could become heinous, that the little stubble of facial hair foretold a future of more fear and heartache. Over and over, she reviewed her relationship with him and tried to analyze it for clues to explain his behavior. She had known that hurdles lay ahead the day of his arrival when he refused the cookies bubbling with melted chocolate. He did not drink milk. He wanted Coke. He didn't like cookies; he liked cigarettes. He liked "the weed" so much he stole a package of Winstons from Ed Burrough, a next-door neighbor, the first week he was in town. The usually mild-mannered Ed went straight to Estelle and accused the boy, telling her, "That kid needs an attitude adjustment. He should be taught a lesson."

She agreed, but all she knew to do for discipline was to use a paddle. When she tried that, he wrestled it from her and warned, "Leave me alone, you old bat." Before long the whole town was referring to "that Trager boy."

Was that it? Should she have tried to punish him? She had spanked his mother when she was a child, and Nadine had never seemed to resent it, had indeed remained remarkably sweet-tempered. But then Nadine had succumbed to alcohol and left the cocoon of her own provincial Southern life, never to return. Maybe she, too, had hated her mother but kept the festering sore hidden. Maybe she had filled her son with her own hostility, only sending him to Alabama out of desperation. "Maybe she's dying of AIDS, wandering in the ghettos of Chicago," she thought. "Did I do that? What might she have told the boy? Did she demonize me? Did she?"

If it was not the attempted punishment, what then? Was it wrong to make children go to worship services? She was appalled when he refused to go after one visit. He couldn't read well enough to participate in the doxology and, thinking Communion silly, he giggled and ate a handful of broken wafers when the minister said, "This do in remembrance of me."

She was mortified and tried to teach him morals and manners in the conventional Christian way. She insisted on saying grace before meals and urged him to memorize "God is great; God is good; let us thank him for our food."

"I got my own blessing," he told her, bowing his head and reciting, "Rub a dub dub; thank you for the grub."

She knew that she should teach him respect, but she failed at this too, and eventually her fantasy of seeing him baptized in a white robe under the cross dimmed and disappeared altogether. She realized finally that she could not persuade or coerce him into being God-fearing. Should she not have tried? If she hadn't, would the dog collar and chains and black clothes have come anyway? Did she give him to Satan?

Or was it really because she was old — a generation so far removed that he was repulsed by everything about her. Before he came, she had not thought that being seventy-five years old was onerous. But when she cataloged herself, she had to admit that the sum of the parts was not pretty. The mass of once vainglorious black hair had thinned so radically that the beautician now had to tease and manipulate it to cover the pink scalp underneath. For comfort and convenience, she kept it short and tried to buy clothes to compliment iron gray hair and to disguise the bulges that came with weight gain. Was he disgusted by her sagging breasts that no bra could adequately accommodate? By the spindly legs so out of proportion to her thick thighs and enormous stomach? By the roan-colored age spots that polka-dotted her hands and arms and by the spidery varicose veins of her legs? He had laughed hurtfully at first sight of her poor collapsed mouth without dentures. He had mocked her when inner ear trouble made her hold to the walls and furniture in order to stay upright and move. Once when she had forgotten to bag a soggy Depends, he came from the bathroom, holding it by the corner yelling, "Hey, have a little respect for the kid." She had spent fifteen thousand dollars to build a private bathroom for him. After all the years of solitude and privacy, she felt pinned under a microscope, with all of her physical flaws magnified and made gross. Was she gross in the eyes of a teenager? Had he respected his mother? His father? Who was his father anyway? A dope addict? Perhaps the hatred came from his father's genes, and it was not her fault at all. She clung to that.

She confided in her pastor, who advised her to pray and read the Bible. She prayed, but her pain only ballooned into a kind of mental gangrene. The Bible told her that the meek would inherit the earth, but she inherited only rue. Once, on a wild impulse, she told him that she loved him. But he rewarded her by stealing and wrecking her car. When she refused to pay bail for his release from jail, his bitterness swelled into a stream of obscenities that offended even seasoned criminal inmates. He threatened to kill her when he got out.

He stayed in jail for thirty days and came home silent and sullen. They did not speak, and one morning when she awoke he was gone. She knew he would be back because nothing was missing from his room. She settled into her recliner to enjoy a mug of hot tea and fantasized about what her life would be without him. The peace and serenity would be more precious than winning the Publishers Clearing House Sweepstakes. As if walking inside the bubble of that fantasy, she finished her tea and dressed for town in her most becoming outfit, a beige jacket dress in the new longer length. She completed her ensemble with dangly earrings in a deep coral shade to match her tank top. She felt pleasurably decadent, and her mood lifted when she looked into a mirror and knew she was not gross. She reached for her brown canvas purse on the dresser. It wasn't there. She searched for an hour, knowing that she wouldn't find it. He had stolen money from her before, but he had never taken her purse. Tired and shaken, she walked out to the porch and sat on the steps.

"Is this your purse, Miss Estelle?" It was Ed, calling to her from the sidewalk in front of her house.

"It looks like it, Ed. I've been hunting it."

Ed approached, holding it gingerly.

"Where did you find it?" she asked.

"It was in the street down there at the curve," he said, handing it over. "I thought it looked like yours."

It felt heavy and damp, and the foul smell it exuded filled her with foreboding. She thanked Ed and took the purse. Already suspecting what was inside, she wanted to seal the purse in a garbage bag and throw it away. But she had to retrieve her billfold and papers.

Setting it on the kitchen counter near the sink, she unzipped it and reeled from the stench of excrement and urine. Her hairbrush, Cover Girl makeup, Kleenex, and billfold sloshed in the wet mess. She retrieved her empty wallet, social security check, and visa card with the kitchen tongs. The card was plastic and thus unharmed. The only legible thing on the check was "pay to the order of." When she thought *"pay to the order of shit,"* she laughed out loud and realized she might be hysterical. Sickened by the smell, she mused, *"This is your life. Just a purse full of feces."* He had threatened to kill and she had lived in terror. But this last development was intolerable and she could never forgive him, blood or no blood.

The future had betrayed her, denied her its promise of rainbows. The present was a slough of despondency. Where could she go but to the past? She had thought she could not open that iron door, but she was wrong.

It opened, swung wide, on the day of the purse incident when the azaleas and the dogwoods were blooming in pink splendor in her front yard and a beautiful little neighbor girl with golden curls came to her porch with a bouquet of violets tied neatly with a white ribbon.

"I thought you might like them, Miss Estelle," she said timidly.

She took them, breathed deeply of the scent, and squeezed the child's hand. "Thank you, Love," she said and watched the curls bounce back down the walk. She sat down in the swing and it was 1931 again, the heart of the Depression. She was twelve years old, too big for the blue and pink flour-sack dress that stretched tightly over her budding breasts. She was on her knees in a grove of pine trees, her hands framing an icon of a tuft of wild violets. They were exquisite, too perfect to be touched. "*A bunch of blueness*," she thought, and the phrase lay like honey on her tongue. She carried the musical sounds of it with her, singing in her brain, as she left the little bower and hurried down the primitive dirt road that connected her home a mile away to the county road. The absence of trees along this stretch of road added to the July heat that scorched the soles of her bare feet. She hurried along, afraid now that she might have missed her weekly rendezvous with the rolling store.

Then she rounded the last curve, and her heart lifted at the sight of the vehicle, a big red Ford truck colorfully embellished and loaded with a wonderland of goods so precious that few in the crowd gathered there could buy. It was their mobile miniature store, traveling every Tuesday the twenty miles from the nearest town and carrying almost everything necessary to surviving in a time of almost hopeless deprivations. It had been so long ago, but she could see the crowd that day as though it were yesterday.

Poor Will Bigby, his dirt-caked overalls drooping on his thin frame, had left his field to come trade a Rhode Island Red hen for a file with which to sharpen his hoe. Rose Ann, with her eight-month-old son straddling her hip, fingered the bolts of fabric and longed for a dotted Swiss dress. She sighed and settled for a new spool of white thread, resigned to using the flour sack material she had saved. Mrs. Childers was there with her basket of eggs to trade for sugar and flour. When Mr. Trager told her that she didn't have enough eggs for both, she reluctantly put the sugar back, her eyes downcast and smoldering with resentment.

Next to church, the rolling store gathering was the social event of every week, and on that day she stood, as always, on the fringe, separated from the people of the farming hamlet by her shyness, the absence of a mother in her life, and the social alienation of a father who didn't know how to farm and spent his time making nets and fishing. Often hungry, she was drawn to the rolling store, although she never had anything with which to buy or barter.

On that eventful day, she drew close to the crowd, caught up in the excitement of the children, all of whom it seemed were cashing in on a money-making venture which she had known nothing about. For weeks, they had scoured the woods, scraping resin from sweet-gum trees into syrup buckets for a glue manufacturing company. Parents had confiscated most of the children's money, leaving them only a small amount for candy. They were giddy with happiness, jostling for a good view as Mr. Trager opened the candy display. There were red and white peppermint sticks, pink gummy slices, and orange peanut-shaped candy. And then she saw the bars of coconut candy with their white, yellow, and red stripes. A wave of gustatory desire swept over her, reminding her of the time Jamie had given her a small pinch of his coconut candy bar. The children made their choices, and the hubbub quieted as they solemnly, slowly enjoyed the rare pleasure. She had watched, mesmerized, as Jamie nibbled at his coconut bar, and she felt dizzy from desire. When he turned to take a lick off his sister's peppermint stick, a little corner of his candy fell off into the dirt. And she had impulsively picked it up, brushed it off, and eaten it. Barely had she swallowed it when she looked up to see Mr. Trager watching her. Overcome by shame and her need and her weakness, she fled.

Her little bower welcomed her, offered her the violets as a substitute for the forbidden fruit of candy. But she could not forget the taste of the candy, even with grains of dirt, which had left the bitter taste of shame lying like gall on her heart. She lay on the grass, face towards the violets, and fantasized that the bunch of blueness had been left on her pillow by a beautiful young boy with angelic blonde curls. She closed her eyes and willed herself into an escapist sleep, seeking closure to the desperate hollowness of a life tortured by cruel need.

When she roused later, she was not looking at the violets but into the remarkable blueness of Edgar Trager's eyes as he squatted beside her. She was not alarmed, sensing that she was in the presence of kindness. "Look," she said, pointing to the flowers, "They're like your eyes."

And with that, she walked out of the Depression and into Edgar Trager's heart. The economy continued to be miserable, but they sustained each other. Born with a bone deficiency, he had limped through life, bracing himself through a lonely childhood of bullying and ridicule. Twice as old as Estelle, he forgot his clumsiness with his social peers and pleasured in her respect and admiration. From that first encounter, when his compassion made him bring her the coconut candy, their relationship grew from friendship into the romance of clandestine courtship, and when she turned thirteen, he could wait no longer and asked her for sex. The little bower shielded them, under a canopy of green, from the judgmental eyes of the Primitive Baptist community, and Mother Nature looked on, not confused about the relevance of sex to love. They had fumbled through the sexual experience, the first one for both, to discover a passion that was to buoy them through the rest of the Depression.

Revisiting those years now, Estelle had to re-evaluate the deep psychological scars of that time which had crusted on her soul like leper's sores. From a new perspective, the past horror of hunger and the colossal deprivation dimmed and disappeared into images of beauty in the bloom of violets and warm blue eyes, of sweetness in the tenderness of masculine arms cradling her in lovemaking, of the wrenching empathy of her husband's tears at her childbirth agony, of the pure sheen of a delicate little ring presented to her on their fifth anniversary. But most striking of all was a comforting absence — the absence of fear and hatred. She had not been subjected to that during the worst of times; she resolved not to endure it any longer in her old age.

She set the swing in motion, liberated by embracing her past and eager to reclaim the serenity of her old age. She would put her grandson out of her house and life with the courage and strength forged within her by the toughness of her past. As it turned out, she didn't have to do anything. Sheriff Baker walked onto her porch, sat down and removed his sweat-stained, wide-brim straw hat. He told her then that he had taken the boy in for questioning and that the Chicago police would be there the next day to claim him. A young enterprising police detective had cracked a cold case with unassailable proof that Craig had killed her daughter. She took the news with battling emotions — sadness that her child was dead but relief that the sadistic menace had been reduced to zero in her life. Then quickly assaulted by guilt that she had betrayed Edgar's bloodline by turning her back on their grandson, she gave a low moan of grief, "My child, my grandchild."

The sheriff rose. "No ma'am," he said. "Not your grandson, Miss Estelle. Your daughter had no children. He was just a smart-mouth punk with a killer instinct, prowling the streets and conning people like your daughter. He killed her — you don't want to know how ma'am — got her papers and showed up here pretending to be your grandson. Don't waste no pity on him. He's just pure-dee evil, a bad seed if I ever saw one."

And the law officer was mercifully gone. She watched him pull into the street and disappear. Moments later, she too left, parking at a fresh produce stand uptown. She was on a redemptive mission, which involved a big sack of purple hull peas.

The Renaissance Man

WHAT Screamersville needed to get through the Depression, Judge Scoggins decided, was a Renaissance man. It was expressed as a joke, but his son, called Junior by everyone who knew him, took it seriously and declared that he would be that Renaissance man.

First, he prowled through some relevant books in his father's law library and came away from his research with a vague idea of great multi-talented iconic figures who wowed the rich Medici in sixteenth-century Italy. He could be Michelangelo and Shakespeare and a doctor and a preacher if that's what the hard times required.

Now in his late twenties, he was generally considered to be a rustic dilettante. His father thought him brilliant but would admit to his being "different." Once, in a truth-serum mood, he had speculated that Dr. Morgan had circumcised the wrong part of his son's anatomy.

The first person with whom Junior shared his vision of himself in a new role was Miss Rosa Appleby, the retired schoolteacher spinster, who listened to him in amusement and pointed out that he had no credentials for such a lofty aspiration and that the Sistine Chapel was awesome but could not put food on the table.

He was not one whit discouraged, remembering his childhood as an artist and businessman. He recalled his habit of doodling on everything, a practice which his mother praised. It led him to raid the attic to rescue some of the old drawings. One of them, a sketch of the old courthouse with its two massive Corinthian columns, was, he decided, a bit amateurish but showed promise. He remembered then that his childhood ambition to be an artist had resulted in his and Craig Smith's operating a vending stand to sell his art. The venture had been short-lived because he had served his customers drinks from his father's liquor cabinet. He knew that the liquor had been made at Runt Wilson's still in the woods behind Pete's Pond out in the country, but the brew was tempting as it lay like liquid diamonds in his mother's heavy crystal decanter. He and his customers had become tipsy and wallowed in a pleasant glow until somebody told the judge and ruined the enterprise.

Now here he was, caught in the deprivations of a national depression, with a lingering regret over the loss of artistic talent that might have elevated him to the status of a savior figure in Screamersville. A struggling little town in the Alabama Black Belt, it had kept its pioneer name that reflected the wildness of its early history. The town was tame now. Gone were the gun battles, saloon stabbings, and the wails of women in the night. But as the Depression relentlessly pushed the people into poverty, there was a sense of screaming, silent but boiling, just under the surface of everyday life. Although Junior's own personal life as the son of the town's most powerful and respected family was less threatened than others, he felt the pain and desperation of their lives.

His thoughts turned to writing. He knew that he could not be Shakespeare. But he liked to write, and he had liked the saying that the pen is mightier than the sword. He knew that he could write because he had a publication to his credit. He had entered an essay contest in *Grit Magazine* and won second place with his portrayal of his life as the son of a distinguished judge. His father tried to be proud but was embarrassed at the self-conscious erudition, the piling on of polysyllabic words like "magnanimous attitude," "mellifluous voice," and "prognosticative abilities." Back he went to recover the old yellowed magazine from the attic. Reading it again after all those years, he winced at the hey-look-at-me diction and wondered why he had ever thought he could write.

So he took his plan for being a Renaissance man back to the drawing board and determined to use his artistic instincts as a broad humanities base on which to build a career as a doctor. Surely that profession would allow him the opportunity to do enormous good in a chaotic time of great need.

The next semester at the University of Alabama found him in chemistry and physics classes, which he hated, and in an anatomy class, which intrigued him and led him to apprentice himself to a friend of the Judge, a Tuscaloosa doctor with a practice in gynecology. A sense of euphoria settled over him as he trailed his doctor mentor through office visits, examinations, diagnoses, surgeries, and home visits. And he developed a special relationship with Matilda, Dr. Strait's wooden mannequin, a shapely full-figured form with intricate anatomically correct insides.

With a keen scientific interest, he studied the coiled intestines, the stomach, the colon, kidneys, liver, appendix — all painted a ghastly pink, which he admired in the belief that the color fairly represented the look of real organs. He was excited to learn about female genitalia, which had been a fascinating mystery to him. The positioning of the womb, the fallopian tubes, the ovaries, the vagina and the clitoris became emblazoned on his mind like a map.

The magic of reproduction stirred in him a purely medical interest, but there was nothing scientific about his feeling when Matilda was all closed up, and the seductively curved hips and the rounded breasts reminded him of Melly Landers. The memory of Melly fired his imagination with a lust that burned even brighter as he watched Dr. Strait examine his patients' breasts.

The elderly doctor, encouraged by Junior's eager interest, seized the opportunity to teach and demonstrated the procedure for feeling a woman's breasts to detect lumps that might be cancerous. It was the first time Junior had heard the word "cancer," and he listened intently to the doctor's explanation that women were vulnerable to breast cancer, which was most often fatal. He impressed upon his young assistant how important it was to detect the disease in its early stages in order to save lives.

The phrase "save lives" suggested a role for the Renaissance man as a savior figure. He could not have been more inspired if a heavenly chorus had called to him with the summons to "Go forth." Under Dr. Strait's watchful eye, Junior performed several breast exams and felt buoyed by the veteran doctor's praise. The light bulb in his brain blazed with a sudden conviction. He would be a breast examiner specialist. To that end, he purchased a black bag, a stethoscope, needles and syringes, tongue depressors, a blood pressure apparatus, cotton balls, bandaging gauze, rubbing alcohol, and a watch with a second hand. To make himself look slightly older, like a reputable physician, he bought a pair of thick lens glasses and applied white shoe polish to the edges of his hair. When his image in the mirror assured him that he looked trustworthy, he set off for Fifteenth Street.

He chose his first house carefully, stopping in front of a modest little white wooden house with neat green shutters, a brick walk, and blooming azaleas splaying a pink glow everywhere. He almost lost his nerve when no one answered his knock immediately and was about to turn away when a thin young woman wearing a becoming blue gingham dress opened the door.

"Good morning," he said, with what he hoped was his most engaging smile. "I'm Leonard Armstrong, one of Dr. Martin Cox's medical students at the University. I'm working on a project that I would like to talk with you about. May I come in?"

She was puzzled and a little reluctant, but she did let him in and listened to his carefully prepared speech.

"I know it must seem strange," he said, "to have a doctor make a house call without being summoned. But I assure you this is a perfectly legitimate clinical research project conducted by interns under the supervision of the medical college. The study has been commissioned by the state health department in the interest of locating and identifying women with breast cancer in order to treat it early on and save lives.

He could tell she was uncomfortable. "I don't know what cancer is," she said, her cheeks going slightly pink.

"That's understandable. Women have been dying for years with this disease without knowing what was wrong with them." He did the best he could with describing symptoms and treatment, emphasizing the importance of being examined and evaluated early.

"What do I have to do?" she asked.

"Three things. I'll take your vital signs, help you fill out a medical history form, and then examine your breasts — the same as in a doctor's office."

"I don't have money to pay you." She seemed ashamed.

"The service is absolutely free. We know that the Depression is keeping people from needed medical care."

With his little black bag, the professionalism of a real doctor, and the quiet cooperation of his patient, he undertook the examination. He pulled an unsteady chair beside the bed where she lay with her dress open and was caught in the snares of his dueling impulses: The perfection of the breasts registered in his mind as seductive beauty, but any arousal was kept at bay by his unexpected empathy for the patient, who was even younger than he. Her body language—the rigid stillness of her body, the turning away of her face, and the refusal to look at him—made him keenly aware of her painful embarrassment, her struggle to endure the violation of her privacy to get peace of mind about her health. When his hands began their exploratory movements, she closed her eyes, and a little frown creased her brow. His fingers were immune to lust as he silently commanded himself not to find any lumps. When he was finished, she sat up, buttoning her dress, and asked, "Am I all right, Doctor?"

"You're just perfect. No suspicious knots or lumps."

She smiled then, her lips trembling ever so slightly and her green eyes dancing in the happy color of spring. "I'm so relieved," she admitted. "I was worried about the baby."

In amazement, he watched her pat her absolutely flat stomach. "You're going to have a baby?" he asked.

"Yes," she said happily. "When you told me about cancer, I was so afraid that I might not be able to nurse the baby."

"How far along are you?"

When she told him six months, he expressed concern over her lack of weight gain and urged her to eat more.

"Oh, I have always been skinny," she told him brightly. "I get enough to eat. We have a good little garden in the back yard."

He was skeptical, but the irrepressible joy she felt over her maternal expectations gave his own spirits a lift. He philosophized that the little china doll of a woman, so fragile and pretty, would defy the Depression, meet hardship with tough love, and glory in her woman's role of reproduction. He thought her to be beautiful — truly innocent and brave. Reluctantly he left her, but he had the names of several women in the neighborhood who might be interested in participating in the study.

At the end of the extraordinary day, he felt fulfilled. On one level, he knew very well that he was a con man who would be exposed and punished eventually. But on another level, he knew that his behavior, though originally deriving from impure motives, was a sincerely noble attempt to save lives. Not once had he thought of the voluptuous Melly.

But she forced her way into his dreams that night, clawing viciously like a yowling cat at his face while he tore at her clothes to get at the wicked breasts whose image had tormented his libido for months. Walking her home after prayer meeting, he had caved in to potent sixteen-year-old urges, and in the shadow of the church he tried some ill-advised moves which sent her into near hysteria. He awoke in a sweat and did not understand why the image that remained in his mind was the church steeple.

For the next month he accumulated a lifetime's worth of images that bedeviled his mind sleeping and waking. While he honed his skills as pseudo-physician, his memory bank bulged with experiences that brought the Depression up close and personal. More bitter than quinine was the plight of Mildred LeGrande, who opened the door to his knock, grabbed his hands and pulled him in eagerly.

Mistaking him for an undertaker, she led him directly to a bedroom, where the only piece of furniture was a handsome four-poster bed burdened with the lifeless body of her husband. A petite woman with black hair pulled severely back into a bun, she had the flawless delicate look of a porcelain doll and moved with practiced grace. She called him monsieur and spoke with an accent, asking him what information he required. When they both realized that theirs was a case of mistaken identity, he explained that he had been called to a different patient in the neighborhood and got the wrong address. The mistake made him uneasy, and he wanted to leave, but she begged him to stay, "Just until the funeral people come, monsieur. It is just that I am afraid to be alone with the dead."

He reassured her. "I think you are a brave person. You have bathed and dressed him, and look at the careful way you have brushed his hair." And they stood and stared down at the corpse, a handsome man with black hair tinged with gray and an elaborately curved handlebar mustache.

"You think I did good, Monsieur?"

"Yes, indeed."

With the intimacy that could only be understood by lovers, she leaned down and stroked the cold cheek of her dead love and murmured in a silken whisper. "Now I dance for you, ma cheri, the last time."

With that, the black-clad figure rose on tiptoes in her steel-toed ballet shoes and raised her arms above her head in an arc. With no music but the memories in her head, she danced in celebration of the joy and sorrow of her life. Her audience had no trouble imagining that the beginning of the dance, with its quick, fluid movements and the happy expression on the dancer's face, represented the meeting of the lovers in the shadow of the Eiffel

Tower during the Great War. Then the movements suggested the "Wedding March," with the tiny hands pulling love out of the air and holding it over her heart. He lost the thread of her story then and gave himself over to the beauty of the dance with its magic. He did not want it to end, but the dance slowed into the sense of funereal march as the expressive hands and arms reached upward as if giving up the loved one to eternity.

Spent, she stood at the foot of the bed and spoke: "*Au revoir, ma cheri.*" The ruffled sheer fabric at her neck rose and fell. Her eulogy had not been macabre; it had produced an emotional power that moved both of them.

"Please to come with me now, Monsieur Doctor," she urged, taking his hand and leading him through the door, which she closed with a click of finality.

In the living room, standing in a pool of October sunlight, she looked older, he thought, noting the fine lines around her mouth and eyes. He watched her walk to a scarred brown suitcase sitting beside the front door and change to a pair of sensible black walking shoes. A strange sense of emptiness emanated from the oppressive space around him, unoccupied except for a massive breakfront at one end of the room. It was much more elegant than the one in his own home. Seeing him studying the piece of furniture, she took from it the only thing there — a sterling silver statuette of a young ballerina.

"For my role in the National Ballet's performance of *The Nutcracker*," she explained, holding it to her chest like a baby. "The ballet was the heart of my life until a handsome young American soldier showed me what real happiness is," she confided. "We were happy, even though his life took him into the mines to earn a living." Then bitterness claimed her voice. "The mine controlled our lives until it closed, and then the Depression came and it was the beginning of the end. *C'est la vie.*"

He was too awkward with words to know how to comfort her. "What will you do now?"

The question stirred within her the hatred of implacable foes that could not be grappled with in fair fight. Her voice was a vicious claw: "America is a lie. It promises the dream, then kills it. I think God does not love America, or else why would he send this cruel Depression. I say the Lord's Prayer and choke on my anger."

Suddenly, she was reciting the first phrases of the prayer in French. She spat out the words in contempt, her face contorted and her gray eyes enormous: "*Notre Père qui est aux cieux/ Que ton nom soit sanctifité/ Que ton règne vienne.*" His ego swelled at her assumption that he would understand French.

She shifted into English for the words "Thy will be done," words that she now clearly despised. She flung her fury into the empty room, crying, "*Mon Dieu, Mon Dieu*, why was it your will? Why? He was my world." Her passionate orgy of grief reverberated in the mausoleum of a room.

He was relieved when the undertaker knocked and brought back into focus the mundane world with its insistence on getting the dead satisfactorily buried. "I'm Walter Boswell, with Fleet's Mortuary, Mrs. LeGrande. If you will just show us the deceased."

Made calm by their appearance, she busied herself with assisting them, and when the stretcher with its burden left the house, she picked up the suitcase and they followed the corpse to the waiting hearse. As the door closed, she called, "*Dieu vous garde, ma chéri.*"

"Where are you going?" he asked as the hearse moved away from the curb.

"I go home to France, Monsieur Doctor. *Au revoir.*"

He watched her stride purposefully down the street. He would see her in his dreams, striding away down the street or performing her dance of death with consummate grace.

Many disturbing scenes intruded into his sleeping and waking hours. He might be in the process of examining a breast and find himself thinking of the woman with the goat. He had walked into her house with his black bag and found himself confronting the Depression face to face in the form of four barefooted, ragged, big-eyed children so malnourished they moved in a cloud of lethargy. The woman herself was a ghost of a human, clutching a newborn baby, which cried weakly and gnawed its fist.

He forgot his purpose in response to her overwhelming need. "Is there anything I can do for you?" he had asked.

A faint tic worried the corner of her flat lips. "Do you know how to milk a goat?" she asked, clearly expecting nothing. "I can't nurse the baby, and somebody gave me a nanny goat."

He would have tried anything. "Well, I have milked a cow, so I'd be glad to try. Where is the goat?"

The tallest child, a ten-year-old with a grotesque harelip, left the room and was back immediately, leading an uncooperative animal with a full udder in desperate need of milking. It eyed the doctor with a malevolent yellow glare and chewed mightily on a piece of brown paper bag.

"Get me a pan with some water and a pail for the milk," he directed the boy. The child moved quickly to the kitchen and returned with the water and pail. The children eased forward to watch the drama. "Put the halter around her neck, stand in front of her, and try to make her stand still," he told the boy.

"She'll butt me," the reluctant child said.

"Maybe. But the baby needs milk." And with that, he went to his knees, held the pan of water under the goat and washed each teat carefully.

"Aah," the boy said, finally understanding and relishing his role at center stage.

With the mother hovering behind him to watch, he showed them how to pull on the teat, occasionally pushing a teat upward into the udder for a better flow of milk. When he got the milk squirting into the pail with a regular rhythm, the children were amazed, and the mother urged him to let her try.

The goat, no doubt relieved to be rid of her overload of milk, behaved well, and the mother was just as relieved that she had learned how to get the precious milk.

Junior prepared to leave, thinking wryly that he would be forever cured of his fascination for breasts, having found no sexual excitement whatsoever in a goat's teats.

The pathetic little group followed him to the door with gratitude for the miracle of milk. But they scattered frantically with the shriek of "Nanny goat is eating the Bible."

He could find no humor or hope in another instance when he had to attend to an immediate need. Someone had given him the name of Gloria Pettway, who lived in the Forest Hill subdivision on the west side of town. When he explained his mission, she agreed readily, but she made it clear that she expected a quid pro quo. A dumpy little woman in her sixties, she had a round face and a sweet smile which was affixed to her face like a psychic signature. She smiled through the medical history forms, through vital signs (even when told that her blood pressure was 185 over 95) and through the examination. She was indifferent when he found no signs of cancer. Her purpose clearly was the fulfillment of the promise of a favor he had agreed to.

Buttoning her housecoat, she led him to a bedroom. It was dominated by a hospital bed in which resided a huge grown man, perhaps forty years old. Nothing moved except his eyes. Her smile broadened as she kept up a croon: "Here we are, precious. Everything will be all right now. Mama's here. The doctor is here and the world is good. Are you hungry, little one? Soon Mama will feed you strawberries and cream if you are good for the doctor. And you will be good, won't you? You are your mama's precious one, the apple of her eye." All the while she chattered she was stroking his cheek, brushing his hair back from his forehead, wiping the saliva from a corner of his mouth, smoothing the sheet over his mound of stomach and immobile legs.

Junior was troubled at the thought that she would expect him to do something medical for the man. But such was not the case. She motioned for him to join her at the bedside. "This is Doctor Leonard, Luv," she said to her son. "He's going to shave you today, pet. Isn't that wonderful? You know, Mama has always said the Lord giveth and the Lord taketh away. Well, the Lord took our dear Mr. Chambers, but see, He has given us Doctor Leonard." She turned to Junior, and the baby talk gave way to her adult voice as she showed him the table containing the items for shaving. There were an antique Wedgewood bowl and pitcher, a shaving mug containing soap and a well-worn brush, a bath cloth and towel, a bib, a straight razor and the leather strop for sharpening the razor. While she put the bib on the patient, Junior checked the long dull blade of the razor and began slapping it against the leather strop. Almost immediately, the patient reacted to the slapping sound. It began as a low guttural moan and grew into the primitive sound of a wounded animal. The flesh of his face had the bloated look of a balloon.

When Junior looked at the woman for some explanation, she smiled her answer across the room. "Don't be alarmed. He always does that."

"What is wrong with him?"

"He was born an idiot."

"How long has he been invalid?"

"All of his life. I have been blessed." And the smile did not waver.

When the slapping noise stopped, the man's sounds subsided. After Junior had wet and lathered the face, he reached for the razor and held it up to the light to check on the sharpness.

"Don't," she said.

"What?" he asked, but then he saw the man's eyes. Enormous and protuberant, the gray eyes glistened and flamed out in terror, bespeaking a primal fear, desperate and wild.

"Why is he so afraid?"

"He associates the razor with pain. Mr. Chambers was so good to us, but his hands trembled and sometimes he cut Lane."

With that information, his own hands were none too steady. He tried not to look at the terrified eyes, but the fear was so palpable he was drawn into the terror. He felt the pain as though it were his own when the distraction of the eyes caused him to nick the jawline under the thick, stiff stubble. Then he was dealing with blood and lather, as well as the turbulent agitation of the bulging eyes following him.

The mother ministered to the stormy-eyed creature. She picked up his hand and kissed it, saying "Sh, sh, sh" in a low, quieting tone. "It'll be all right. The doctor made a mistake. He's sorry, Luv. He's almost finished, and you're looking so handsome."

Finally it was over and he escaped. But he couldn't keep the image of those feverish wild eyes out of his mind. He never wanted to go through that again. In fact, he had begun to question his mission to save lives through cancer detection. And then something happened to make him rethink his effort to be a Renaissance man.

One day he stopped his car in front of the shabbiest house in a shabby neighborhood, mentally weighing the yard's oppressive mass of overgrown vegetation smelling of dank heat and pelting rain. Azaleas intruded on hollies, Lady Banks roses ran rampant, clogging a rotting flowerbed, and a camellia bush struggled to birth a delicate pink bloom. It was as if the Depression had turned the landscape into a wasteland. Debris and fallen oak leaves littered the ground. The scene mirrored his own psychic twilight. "Drive on, fool," he told himself, but he trudged on toward the door as if challenged, one more time, to test his fate.

With foreboding, he knocked loudly on the paint-peeling derelict of a door. When a woman opened it, he thought of her as a human derelict. Tall, at almost six feet, she had the skin tone of a consumptive, iron-gray hair, and yellow green eyes that looked as if they had seen hell fire. She was emaciated, but her gauntness could not hide the swollen, bloated look of her body. Even her face looked puffy. When she let him in, he was struck by an ominous silence, but he plunged ahead with the sudden conviction that it might be his last chance to save a life.

She listened to him mutely, fidgeting with a torn ruffle on her stained apron. When he had finished, she ventured a timid "Does it hurt?"

"Do you mean the examination or the cancer?"

"Both," she replied.

"Well, the exam won't hurt. In fact, if you pay attention to the way I examine you, you can do it yourself in the future."

"But the cancer?"

"You may not feel pain initially, but pain will come and worsen as the disease advances."

Her eyes clouded as though she didn't know how to proceed. "Do you want me to lay down, or…"

And then, to his consternation, that still silence that he had mistrusted migrained into an explosion as a huge lumberjack of a man leaped from a high wing back chair that had concealed him from view, positioned as it was with the back toward the living room. He had evidently listened to the conversation with his blood boiling. In two strides, he was confronting them, his shaggy rust-red hair falling over one bloodshot eye and his soiled khaki pants unzipped over a ballooning belly.

He tore into his wife first, jerking her to face him and slapping her with a force that reddened her pale face. "Can't wait to jump in bed, can you? I have to beat hell out of you to get you in bed and here you are, ready to spread your legs for any peckerwood that comes along."

She mustered courage enough to defend herself. "He's a doctor," she exclaimed. "I'm sick and you won't take me to a doctor."

He raised his hand again. But he ridiculed her instead. "You got to be the dumbest woman ever lived. A guy shows up in a white coat carrying a black bag and you believe he's a doctor. Before you know it, he'll be selling you the Brooklyn Bridge."

When he turned to Junior, he was a fireball of redneck fury. "You ain't a bit more a doctor than I am a angel. Why ain't nobody heard of this so-called program from the health department?"

Junior was not macho in the best of times, and he was shamefully intimidated, but he stood tall and thrust out his chest, hoping that it would not cave in from the big man's fist. "We're in a Depression. There was just not enough money for the health department to mail out notices. This is a legitimate program, and if you touch me I'll have the police on you so fast it'll make your head spin."

The man balled his fist, and Junior braced himself for a blow. But it didn't come. The woman placed her hand on the fist and said calmly, "No, Jason. You'll go to prison if you're arrested again."

The fist remained clinched, but the man did not swing. Instead, he hit Junior with a barrage of cursing and invective so vicious it would have stopped an eighteen-wheeler in overdrive. He ended his diatribe with a triumphant slur: "Now get yore sorry ass out of my house, coming in here like God's gift to women with the gall to mess with a man's wife's titties. You a poor excuse for a man."

And Junior was about ready to agree with him. Any momentary Alamo kind of bravado had turned into sincere regret that he had ever donned a white coat and tried to save a life. Right then, all he wanted was to save his own skin from a shellacking. To that end, he accepted the man's invitation to leave, and he did so without qualms about valor and honor. The man slammed the door after him with a jar that rattled the hinges.

Junior was halfway to his car when the woman called to him. She rushed down the path to him, saying breathlessly, "Please come back tomorrow. He won't be here. Please, please."

He could not resist her pleading and obvious terror and reluctantly agreed to return.

That night, nightmares torpedoed his sleep as he struggled to free himself from a vast spider web coated with a dark syrup as sticky as glue. Awake in the bright glare of a sun trying to warm a cold November day, he pretended sleep until his roommate left for classes. Sitting on the side of his bed, shivering in the unheated room, he reviewed his situation and ultimately reached the conclusion that he had to go to the woman. He refused to think of the possibility that his nemesis might be there.

She let him in with the quick reassurance that Jason would not be at home until night. He had mercifully found a small job.

With both feeling uncomfortable in the clandestine nature of their meeting, they quickly filled out the form with her supplying the information and him writing it down. Her name was Amanda King and he was jolted to learn that she could not write her name. The X on the line for her signature was like a mute sigh of grief. He ached for her in her naked embarrassment.

Her vital signs were all over the place, danger signals in every negative reading. How could he possibly help her? How to rescue her from a pending stroke? Heart attack? The TB he suspected or the ritual abuse by a madman husband? Her needs were so great and pervasive that he approached the breast examination with dread. He had examined the breasts of thirty-two women, and with each one he shared their elation at the absence of cancer. But this time he knew in his heart that the odds were against a successful outcome. She lay on the bed, and there was in her posture and in her eyes a childlike innocence, a rare kind of trust. Never did a lover fondle a breast with such devotion as he lavished on his clinical analysis. The flesh yielded to his touch as the fingers tested every inch of tissue without encountering any alien matter. He relaxed, straightened his back, and smiled. She could not read a word, but she could read the message in his smile, and he could read the hope in her eyes.

He moved to the other breast, and almost immediately his finger recoiled from a lump the size of a big plum. With his fingers resting on the spot, he looked at her and realized that she had heard the sound of the death knell. A tear slid gently down her cheek and she turned her face to the wall.

He tried to comfort her, but he was seized with a sense of urgency that propelled him into persuading her to go to a doctor. He had made an accurate diagnosis, but he had no power to save her. So he did the best he could. He took her to Dr. Strait. And there in the little office where he had flirted with Matilda, he confessed in private to his mentor what he had been doing and why.

A man of science with little patience for the vagaries of the psyche, the doctor did not know if this son of his old classmate was a lunatic or a well-meaning eccentric. He didn't waste his time analyzing Junior. Together they did a meticulous examination, which the patient endured with emotionless calm. Dr. Strait gave her a three-month supply of medicine for her high blood pressure and made arrangements to perform a lumpectomy to remove the growth.

Junior paid for the doctor's visit and the pending surgery, then carried her home. She assured him that her grown daughter, who lived nearby, would take care of her during and after the surgery. He gave her a wrinkled twenty-dollar bill and felt guilty that in the end all he could do was to give money. Dr. Strait had been mortified by Junior's perversion of the medical profession, but he had amended his sharp criticism with the declaration that his young apprentice had almost certainly saved a life.

But Junior took little joy in the compliment, knowing that his role as a Renaissance man was over. It seemed to him that the manifold hardships wrought by the implacable Depression were overwhelming. And so he went home to Screamersville, where his parents pretended to believe an invented story that was more probable than the truth.

Daily, for a week, he communed with nature from the bank of Coon's Creek, feeding fat worms on his fishing pole to indifferent catfish. Then the letter came. It contained a hundred dollar bill and a page of explanation. Dr. Strait was returning the money Junior had paid for Amanda's surgery. Jason King had beaten her to death when she told him that she was going to have an operation. The man of medicine did not conceal his bitterness. "Where is God," he wrote, "when such heinous things happen? This damn Depression is going to destroy us all."

The guilt Junior grappled with then sent him to the Bible. He left off fishing and devoured the book, searching for the answer to the question the doctor had flung at him about the existence and compassion of God. His total immersion in the orgy of reading troubled his father, and his mother fed him hot tea with chamomile and repeatedly checked his brow. His reading was a poultice for his painful disquiet, and he gradually reclaimed his faith, which had been anemic at the time of his baptism at age twelve.

He took a break and went back to the creek bank with his fishing pole. He was there primarily to reflect and did not expect to catch anything. But almost immediately his worm-baited line jerked as if a fish had accepted an invitation to dinner. Junior responded with a true fisherman's excitement and hauled up a hefty catfish with its tail flapping desperately. Once he had his hands on the fish, he felt a white calm settle over him. "Hey, fish," he said. "Long time no see." To his amazement, the fish abruptly stopped struggling, and Junior could swear the fish's eye blinked at him.

In a flash, his mind conjured up a scene at the Sea of Galilee where Christ's first disciples, Andrew and Peter, left their trade as fishermen to follow Jesus as fishers of men. Junior recognized his call. "I hear you, God," he assured his creator, thrilling at a surge of power in his voice. He thought of the old prophet Isaiah bowing to his God and saying, "Here I am. Send me." Tenderly he freed the fish from the hook and eased it back into the water.

Then the ex-Renaissance man got the second chance he was praying for when the Baptist minister succumbed to tuberculosis and had to be quarantined. The way was clear for Junior to make his debut on the spiritual stage. His road-to-Damascus moment welled into a rhapsodic messianic conviction that demanded expression. At the Wednesday night prayer meeting, he spoke and prayed with such pious passion that the deacons hired him on the spot to be their interim pastor. His heart was afire with the desire to save souls, an even loftier aspiration than healing the body.

For his first Sunday behind the pulpit, he dressed in his black winter suit with its faint odor of mothballs and slicked down his usually unruly brown hair with hair tonic. He had lost weight, but he felt that his slim frame was totally apropos for the lean times and did not worry about his drooping trousers. He hoped that he looked like a man of God as he sat stiffly on the little pine bench behind the pulpit.

It seemed an interminable time for the prayers to be prayed, for the collection plates to be passed for the meager offerings, and for the ten-member choir to sing praises to the Lord. To his surprise, he discovered that he had a pleasant enough baritone voice and joined in the singing, keeping time with his foot. He came out strong on the "wonder working power" of the "blood of the lamb" and felt invigorated by the old familiar hymns whose lyrics now seemed to him to be poetry of the highest order. Finally, Mr. Otis and Miss Carolyn ended the musical part of the services, and the pulpit was his.

Deliberately, as if on stage, he placed on the stand the Judge's silver pocket watch, assuring the congregation that his sermon would end precisely at twelve o'clock, even if he were in mid-sentence.

To satisfy their curiosity, he assured them immediately that they were looking at a new Junior Scoggins, now a man of God transformed by his call from on high. He judiciously referred only vaguely to the role of the winking catfish as the instrument of divine will.

Swiftly, he moved into the darkness of the Depression blighting their lives. "Look," he instructed, dramatically thrusting his hand toward the bare windows. "That's a bleak gray winter landscape outside, isn't it? It kind of matches the misery of our lives and makes us wonder if things will ever be better. Now, you know me. I'm not a wise man, but I have read the Bible, and I know that God lets bad things happen to good people sometimes. Great thinkers and theologians have written eloquently, trying to explain why this is so. But today I am not going to try to explain why God has allowed us to be subject to such hardship and deprivation. I don't know why Eilean and Raymond's little twin boys were born dead; I don't know why money is so scarce that Mr. Jemmerson had to close the hardware store, or why some of our ladies have had to take in washing.

"I don't know the why of these things. But I don't have to. What we all need to know is what to do about it. Since we are all believers here, we can pray for God to change things. And we know that He will heed our prayers eventually." He leaned toward the podium, gripping it until his knuckles whitened. "But the key to our dilemma right now is to get our mindset right. And the way to do that is first to get rid of the frustration and desperation sent by the devil to snare us into the blazing fires of hell. We've got to be like Christ and say, 'Get thee behind me, Satan!'

"We may be tempted to despair like David crying out that he has eaten ashes like bread and mingled his drink with weeping. And we may have an answering cry of the blood when we remember that poem of the old blind poet where he expresses his anguish that God has taken his sight just when he is on fire to write in service to his God." He changed his lofty, emotional tone for a casual aside. "Now you're probably wondering what Junior Scoggins knows about that great writer John Milton. Well, I don't mean to try to sound learned, but I remembered a poem entitled 'On His Blindness,' from my sophomore literature class at the University of Alabama several years ago. Even as an indifferent underclassman, I was struck by Milton's conclusion in the poem that God doesn't need Milton, that 'they also serve who only stand and wait.' So the great poetic genius learned to wait, and before Milton died he had written those monumental works, *Paradise Lost* and *Paradise Regained*.

"So what we have to do is resist the desperation. We may feel like we have lost our little paradise here in Screamersville, but we can regain it if we keep the faith and wait for God's delivery." Gratified that no one was nodding off, he launched off in the heart of his message, the haunting story of Job, driven wretched by the contest between Satan and God. He discovered, happily, that he could not only sing, but he could act too.

Seized by an impulsive desire to reenact the book of Job, he abandoned his written notes on the pulpit and strode before the congregation. He gave a decent impersonation of the majestic God and a convincing portrayal of a strutting Satan proclaiming that he had come "from going to and fro in the earth and from walking up and down it." He managed some rustic drama in the initial conflict in which God accepted Satan's challenge to test Job. Then he was first one and then the other of the messengers who reported the calamities that befell Job. He gave short shrift to the dialog of the three false friends, having found that part of the book tedious and boring.

Mindful of his theme, he depicted Job's joyous reconciliation with God and the restoration of his prosperity. He relished the happy-ever-after ending, emphasizing that Job had kept the faith, had waited and endured unspeakable suffering and was rewarded with a hundred and forty more years of life.

He flipped his Bible open and told them, "We are not as perfect as Job. We are God's children, though, and he will take care of us." Again he consulted his Bible, turning the tissue thin paper to read from Isaiah: "'And therefore will the Lord wait, that he may be gracious unto you... blessed are all they that wait for him.'

"We must wait, you see, and count our blessings." He stopped his measured pacing, planted his feet firmly in front of his listeners and reminded them of the great famine that struck Samaria while they were under siege by the Syrians. "They were so hungry that they would pay fourscore pieces of silver for an ass's head and five pieces of silver for a handful of bird's dung to eat." He paused to let the horror of eating bird's feces sink into their imagination. "Remember the Israelites wandering in the desert for forty years after leaving Egypt? Did God take care of them?" It was a rhetorical question but he was elated at the nodding heads and murmured "yeses." Emboldened by the audience involvement, he posed another question. "And how did God rescue them?" The response was immediate: Like a chorus from an old Greek tragedy came an incantation of "manna from heaven," delivered with Southern Baptist pride in their Biblical knowledge.

He strode behind the pulpit, glanced at the Judge's watch and said, with an audible sigh, "My time is up. But we can all know that god's time is never up. He's always with us, loving us and blessing us when we don't deserve His mercy."

He suddenly realized that he was tired, limp. A trickle of sweat eased from his armpit. From the front row came the tremulous voice of toothless ninety-year-old Chambers Cox: "God is great."

It was the cue for the congregation to ritually end the service: "God is good."

Junior had the last word: "God is great; God is good, all the time." And he dismissed them with a passionate prayer, completely forgetting to offer the traditional invitation to join the church.

But the church treated him with such warmth at leave-taking that he felt as if he had had a transfusion of some kind of manna from heaven.

That buoyant feeling lasted for a few weeks, a time in which he basked in a glow created by a devoted flock who gradually accorded him the respect he had always been denied. He delivered infinite versions of his original message. Under the influence of Junior's spiritual guidance, church members ate their collards and fried fatback, their eggs and grits, without complaint, remembering that things could be worse — they could be eating asses' heads and bird dung.

But a cruelly cold winter broke their spirits, and the optimism waned. People tried to buck up and take care of each other, but there was less and less evidence of God's greatness and goodness.

A story went around that Buddy Mack, the town's homeless black man, had been seen eating corn kernels from cow patties in Mr. Hasty's barnyard. Nobody believed it, but little Cal Adams slipped off from his parents and went in search of the demented old man. He found him frozen dead on the ground, his hand on the door handle of a ruined storm pit. The stiff body was shrouded in icicles hanging from his limbs and from the drooling of the underlip. The sight so unnerved the child that he was left with a permanent stutter.

Chambers Cox deserted his amen pew, trying to avoid pneumonia and the Grim Reaper. Widow Boyd, Chambers' stalwart Christian buddy, apologized to Junior for Chambers' absence, but she, too, succumbed to hardship and soon no longer ventured out. By mid-February, Junior had discontinued the Wednesday night prayer service for lack of attendance. He spent more time digging graves in ice-encrusted ground than in preparing sermons. Again and again, he stood at graveside, often shaking from driving rain and whipping cold wind, trying to give comfort with the ageless words "In my Father's house are many mansions: if it were not so, I would have told you. I go to prepare a place for you."

When he stood beside the clumsily built pine coffin holding little Sally Jane, tortured to death by whooping cough, he quoted Revelations, which promised that "there shall be no more death, neither sorrow, no crying, neither shall there be any more pain." He did not try to analyze why he was more concerned about his wet feet than about the baby's soul. But he did have the grace to feel guilty about it later.

When the consumptive Baptist minister passed away, Junior tried to bury him with spiritual flair and delivered his, "O, death, where is thy sting?" passage in an oration worthy of a Shakespearean actor playing King Lear. This time, when he did not feel guilty over his pretentious performance, he wondered if he might not be spiritually bankrupt.

The weeks stumbled by with unrelenting hardship, and Junior found it increasingly hard to justify the ways of God to man. When the Anse house burned to the ground from live embers in the fireplace ashes Josh Anse had thrown out, the old man hobbled on his club foot to the church steps, where his pastor found him. Clutching a dying yellow cat that smelled of burned flesh, he watched the orange flames lick at the sky and told Junior to take his prayers and go to hell.

The man of God didn't have much better luck with counseling the Barnet brothers, who knifed each other on a regular basis over the issue of who was to blame for the collapse of their sawmill. Junior visited them in jail and appealed to their finer instincts to work for family harmony. But they turned on him, ridiculing his suspect religious conversion and hurling outhouse language and obscene invective at his retreating back.

He felt more and more reluctant to emulate Isaiah's appeal to God to "Send me." And he began to have a strange obsessive feeling that there was malignant evil abroad in the universe. He saw that evil personified in Screamersville in the form of a dark hobo who jumped off a boxcar as the L & N train slowed for the town and then roared away.

The man was the epitome of the feared mysterious hoboes who prowled through towns during the Depression, begging for food and shelter. Slouched into a ragged black overcoat, the man had the hard-bitten look of a prison inmate with his sooty-looking complexion and a scar that whitely slit his thick lips. Junior saw him one day huddled against the locked door of the forsaken hardware store. He would not have been surprised to see cloven hoofs on the man. So he was not surprised (horrified but not surprised) when the nameless menace crashed through the door of Miss Rosa Appleby's house, raped her viciously and forced her to watch him consume everything edible in the kitchen. When Junior visited her later, she was so pitiful that he was conscience-stricken when he had the insane urge to tease her about having been robbed of her greatest antique — her virginity. Not finding "rape" in the concordance of his Bible, he fumbled through some woefully inappropriate Scripture passages and hurried away in confusion and chagrin.

He seized on the idea that Screamersville was in such dire

peril that he could not save it — not as a Renaissance man, a physician, or a preacher. Everywhere he looked, he saw Satan "going to and fro in the earth, and walking up and down in it." He thought that Job's archetypal tester was prancing in glee when he took his mother to see the damage at her late sister's deserted antebellum home. On the day of their visit, the weather seemed bizarre, with still clouds threatening something ominous. Junior remembered that in the Bible a cloud was often the sign of God's presence and protection. Well, he wasn't buying that symbolism in twentieth-century Alabama. The cloud was more likely the work of the devil, he thought.

Rosemount, with its grand hand-hewed Ionic columns, was still the state's best example of Greek Revival architecture and Screamersville's proud symbol of faded glory. The poor whites who had lived in the caretaker's cottage had stripped the mansion of its priceless furnishings and left the house open to the weather and animals. Reba Scoggins stood in the grand ballroom, looked up at the gaping hole where the magnificent chandelier had been, and cried bitterly. "It's a desecration," she lamented.

"Now, Mama," Junior chided. "It's not a temple."

"It is to me," she insisted, peeking into a small parlor. "Oh," she said, a little catch in her throat, "there's where Grandfather kept his Stradivarius." She pointed to a space where a glass display case had held the beloved violin.

But Junior was not tempted into her nostalgia. Preoccupied with the entrance into the magnificent drawing room of a gaunt Jersey cow, his imagination turned the lowing bovine into an image of Satan going to and fro and shitting contemptuously on the Carrera marble floor built with Southern pride.

At sight of the defecating cow, Reba shrieked, but the sound was lost in a cracking and rolling of thunder that shook the ruined edifice.

"We'd better get out of here," Junior yelled at her, but the roaring out of the west was unmistakable. And in the instant in which Junior felt the presence of the old diabolical snake out of the Garden of Eden, the tornado took them.

It dropped them a quarter mile away in a rock-filled gully, his mother hysterical, bruised and cut, and he with a broken leg and tormented by fear of both God and Satan.

He heaved a malevolent rock off his crushed leg and gazed in stupefied wonder at the nearby gaunt cow which had accompanied them on their tornadic journey. There she was, like a bovine cadaver, centered in a spotlight of butter yellow sunshine, chewing a low-calorie cud in slow motion. Just at the moment when the scene seemed to be the epitome of blessed pastoral serenity, the cow hoisted her tail and desecrated God's green earth with just as little regard as she had defaced the marble mansion floor. Junior was sure the cow was a symbol of something mythic, but he couldn't quite figure out what.

After a month of recuperation, he took his fishing pole and theological questions to the bank of Coon's Creek. Spring had slipped in overnight, drenching everything in an avalanche of green, and the sun was pleasantly warm on the back of his neck. He forgot about his colossal spiritual ignorance as the bobbing line enticed him into the warm womb of fisherman's paradise. He examined every catch he hauled in, looking for a God-eyed catfish. Three hours and nine fish later, when no winking fish had summoned him, he came to the conclusion that a fish is a fish, Coon's Creek is not the Sea of Galilee, and a depression is a demonic puzzle.

He knew what he had to do. He went to the church and propped on the pulpit a big sign which read: "It's all smoke and mirrors. I quit. Amen." It was signed "Your pastor, the Renaissance man."

Walking away, he wondered whatever happened to old Melly what's-her-name.

HUNGERS

IF he hadn't been so hungry, he might never have found out. But he was hungry. He was always hungry ever since his Ma left. He didn't have much to eat before she left because his Pa didn't send the family money and didn't stay at home. He didn't know much about his Pa except that he worked for the CCC, and when he came home he'd pull his Ma onto his lap and whisker her, and about the time they all knew there was going to be another baby, he'd go away again. But his being at home didn't make any difference about the family's eating. They didn't have any more when he was there than when he wasn't, so it didn't matter when he left. It didn't matter with his Ma either. He could tell.

Folks said his Ma did better than could be expected without a good man and with so many mouths to feed. She was pretty, and religious, and she went to church every Sunday and made the children go too, even if they didn't have shoes, and she always saw that they had something to eat. His Ma was always good to him. She'd let him go get the poke salit because she said he was a good boy, even if he did have a bad eye, and she knew he'd hurry back. He always did hurry back, and then she'd hug him, and nobody else ever did that.

They always had something to eat before she left. It never was much, but it kept his belly from squeezing together. But then she left, and he was always hungry ever since. He never could remember much about the time right after she left except for being hungry. He was little then, and when he would wake up in the night wanting her and wanting to eat, there was nothing but the darkness, and it followed him through the nights like a big chinaberry tree, and he could feel nothing except the hunger. He would stand in his blackness and swing on the wire fence around the house and watch Mr. Landis ride by on his horse to look at his fields and his cows, and he would remember how the man had used to stop by the fence and talk to his Ma before she left.

And looking at him go by, he could feel the other hunger, the not-belly hunger, and he wanted Mr. Landis to smile and say, "Get up behind me, boy, and we'll ride down to my store and get you a peppermint stick and then you can sleep in my big house and live with me because I miss her, too, and maybe the two of us won't be so lonely." But he never did say it. He never even looked at him or towards the house, and he never again flipped his whip toward him to holler, "Hey, boy," like he used to.

He knew all the time, even in the blackness, there was something he ought to know, to remember about Mr. Landis, but he couldn't, and it made the wanting worse because he thought if he could just remember, then he might be able to make Mr. Landis laugh and sit up straight and he would say, "Hey, boy," and take him home with him. But he could not remember, and so he watched him and waited, and the being hungry was with him all the time.

He did a lot of things to keep from being hungry. Like the funerals. He didn't know why he didn't think of it before, except that for a long time the blackness plagued him so he could not think.

He had never seen as much to eat as there was at old Mr. Hawkins' house when he died. That was the first time he was ever at a funeral. He was just passing the house on the way to town one morning when Mrs. Hawkins came running out into the road, waving her arms and blowing her nose into her apron. The old man had died, she said, and would he go on up to Charlie's house and tell him to fetch the doctor. He did like she said and when he went back to the house folks were gathering. They were crying and shaking hands and asking if so and so had been sent for. He squatted down by the roots of the old hickory tree and watched the women bringing in baskets of fried chicken and potato salad and lard cans of iced tea and milk.

Then they started setting the table for dinner and calling to the men to come eat, as they had to keep up their strength even in time of sorrow, and he went along to the table, too. Nobody noticed him, and he ate and ate. There were so many people; he just stayed around and soon it was supper time and everyone ate again, and after that the friends sat up with the body in the front room and every once in a while some of the women would bring coffee and cake in. The sun came up, and breakfast was served, and then before long dinner was ready. Dinner was the last meal before the funeral, so he sneaked some food into his pockets to take home to Vada. He got some potato salad and some chicken and some of Mrs. Tickey's cake with the white icing that looked like snow flowers. Finally they left with Mr. Hawkins for the church and he went home.

Since then he didn't miss a funeral. Nobody paid him much attention at the wakes and the funerals. Sorrowing folks are different, he found. Those that usually treated him like a dog acted decent and talked soft to him in the death houses.

The rest of the family could look out for themselves, but he had to take care of Vada. He took the snow flower icing home to her, and when she had brushed the pocket trash off, she looked at the scoops of icing and just crumpled up all over with crying.

Then really hard times came. It had been bad for them ever since his Ma left, but then it got to be hard times for everybody, even those that had always eaten high on the hog before. Five-cent cotton and forty-cent meat, they said. Depression, they said.

You'd think in hard times more people would die. But they didn't. One time nobody died for more than four months. Even the old men and the old women chomped their gums and sucked the government's oranges and just wouldn't die. It didn't seem right somehow. He knew Vada couldn't live much longer. But nobody was even sick, so far as he could find out. And it wasn't just in Milton either. He went around to the other towns. But it was just not a time for dying.

Vada got worse and worse. They didn't even have the oranges and prunes and dried beans like the other folks got. The groceries were distributed at the Landis' store because that's where the post office was and because the Landises were the biggest folks in Milton and they were in charge of allowancing it. He guessed that was the reason his family didn't get any. Old Mrs. Landis, with her globby, rutabaga-looking body and her brown spotted teeth and her hating eyes. He felt crushed by her stinginess and hatred.

He remembered the time Mr. Ora did a day's work on her roof. Everybody was standing around in the store when Mr. Ora came in and told her he was through and asked for a box of snuff on credit. She asked him how much he charged for the work, and he said, like he always did, that he didn't charge anything. He always told everybody he worked for that, and then they paid him what they could. He never set a price on his work; that's the way he was. Mrs. Landis knew that, but she acted just like he meant for her not to pay him, and so she said, "Well, much obliged." Then she turned around to Mr. Landis and said, "Don't forget to put that snuff down; he got it on credit."

You could see Mr. Landis's thin, wrinkly-old face get red clear down inside his shirt collar, he was that ashamed of her. He looked at her and said, "I'll be damned, woman. Here the man has done a day's work for you, and you ain't going to pay him a shittin' nickel, then you going to turn right around and charge him for a dime box of snuff. That's a hell of a note." He shuffled out of the store, with her just standing there looking after him with her hate in her eyes.

That's the kind of woman she was. His brother Jed asked her for some of the relief food, but she just said she wasn't wasting the government's food on poor white trash. He didn't know how Mr. Landis could have lived with her all those years, but he did. So far as anybody knew, they got along fine. He guessed that was Mr. Landis' doing though. He always knew he was a good man, even if he couldn't remember that other thing about him. He had heard that at first Mr. Landis had tried to make her quit her penny-pinching ways and stop cheating the farmers, but she was just that way, and he couldn't change her. Perhaps he just got tired of trying after awhile and that's why he had laughed with his Ma across the fence so long ago and now looked so old and lonely.

If Mrs. Landis had been different, he never would have thought about it. Doing it, that is.

He didn't plan to do it. He just thought about it and did it before he could think about something else. It was that quick, but he was never sorry about it. Not while he was doing it or afterwards either.

He looked at Vada lying on the bed that morning and knew it wouldn't be long. She had been too weak to get out of bed for three days. He tried to get her to eat some poke salit, but he didn't have meat or lard to cook in them and she threw up. He even tried to milk Mr. Hawkins' cow while she was out in the pasture, but she wouldn't stand still without her calf, and when he had a little in the bucket, she kicked it all out. He didn't know what to do then.

He went back to the house and got the gun, and Jed said, "You don't think you going to kill nothing, do you?" He said no, but he had to try. They had been trying to scare up some meat from the woods for a long time, but he knew even the rabbits could smell the hunger. There was just one place he hadn't hunted — back of the Landis house. Nobody could hunt there.

He had no call to worry about the shots. He didn't even get a chance to fire at anything. The woods were so still that when he quit walking it seemed as if the whole world had stopped. It was quiet, with the wind far above the treetops. But, God, it was pretty, with little tight curled green buds on the trees and the wet grass thick and soft like water on green velvet cloth. On a slope he lay down on the ground and looked at the rows of redbud trees for a long time without batting his eyes. It was so pretty and peaceful he wanted to die. All in a minute he got tired, so tired he didn't even want to breathe any longer. He didn't want to think about being hungry, or his Ma, or Vada, or Mr. Landis.

It was a good place to die. It would have made the prettiest graveyard in the world. He turned over on his side and pushed his rifle up until it stretched straight out from his forehead. He strained and could reach the trigger. And then he thought about it. If he did it, there would be a funeral and food. The idea just came up out of the green ground under him and rippled through his blood up into his head with a big boom. All of a sudden he felt himself floating above the trees, and he could look down and see his dead self on the clean, damp grass. It seemed as if he had never seen himself before. He had on his army coat as he always did because he was always cold. He didn't know where he got the coat; it seemed as if he had always had it. He didn't remember what it looked like to begin with; now it was yellow-green, slick with dirt. He looked at his big head and his good eye that was red from looking and the one that looked out to the right of him and knew that God must have made him with the scraps left over from other people, the pieces of bone and skin and meat that wouldn't do for anybody else. While he was floating and looking at the rag of himself down there on the grass, he could see it start to rot and the grass around it to shrivel and turn brown.

Then he was back inside himself again with the wet from the grass seeping into him and the gun feeling cold in his hand. It wouldn't do any good for him to do it. In the whole world there was nobody but Vada to have a wake and funeral for him, to be sorry they had mistreated him, to remember him on the cold, rainy nights and to cry because the water would be soaking through the wooden coffin onto him.

But somebody had to die. It was the only way. It ought to be somebody old, somebody who would not miss much of living. He kept on thinking about killing somebody, but he did not really mean to do it.

He got up and went straight up the hill toward the back of

the Landis home. He didn't care if she saw him. He didn't care for anything. He came out of the woods right behind the barn. He heard a shot and the chickens came squawking and running in every direction. They were fluttering and flying low in that way chickens have when they're scared. One of them was running, dead on its feet, with its wing dragging the ground and the blood spurting onto the white feathers. The chicken was blind with dying and never even saw him when it ran head first into his leg, its neck flopping limp on his shoe.

He watched it die, listening to the woman come around the barn. Her steps made a heavy, sucking sound in the wet cow manure. He saw her huge feet, in red rubber galoshes, leave big tracks in the mud when she waddled to the fence. Then he looked up at her. The fat of her was sweating through the cotton print dress she had on, and her bosom was heaving. She had her hair plaited tight about her little head, and her eyes were red, like a pig's.

She looked at him in that hard way and said, "Throw me that chicken."

He shook his head. He didn't know why he did it.

Her face got that purplish red look she always had when she was hating hard. "Don't you dare tell me what you won't do, you filthy, no-count scoundrel. Hand it here."

She stretched out her hand. He didn't move.

She could not get through the strands of the barbed wire fence to come get it. She had to go to the corner and open the gate. She headed toward the gap, grunting, "You're all alike. Lazy, trifling trash, living off other folks. Well, you won't live off me any longer. I'm fed up with the likes of you. Tomorrow I'll have Mr. Landis drive the lot of you off the place. If I'da had my way, you'd been gone long before now. I'll see that you get your just desserts, crazy or no. I've always said you're not half as crazy as you look anyway."

Her voice was low and puffing as she strained at the gate, but he could tell what she was saying. He didn't get mad when she said that about his being crazy. Thinking about it later, he couldn't understand why he didn't get riled up. He didn't know why, but he didn't. Maybe it was because the stillness was all about him again, and he was up in the sky, floating about and looking down on himself and Mrs. Landis coming towards him with Mr. Landis' pistol that she had used to kill the chicken with in her hand hanging down at her side. He was outside himself, watching.

He saw her stoop and pick up the chicken with her left hand, still holding the pistol with her other hand. When she pulled the chicken across his foot, it left a wide bloody streak. Then, as she was straightening up, he took the pistol from her hand and put it to her head and shot her. He saw himself do it, so quick and simple, and still he did not feel anything except that floating feeling as he looked down at her big body on the ground. Her head was no head at all. There was just a big bloody hunk of bone and hair and a few of the little rat-like teeth. Stuff dripped from the low limb of the pine sapling above. He saw himself throw down the pistol and pick up his rifle and the chicken and go around the barn through the strip of pines to the big road and across it through some more woods.

In the woods the floating sensation left him. He was scared some, but mostly he was glad. Maybe now Mr. Landis would be happy again and say, "Hey, boy," and there would be a funeral and big folks and plenty of food. And he had a chicken; it would be good for some soup for Vada.

There was no one home except for Vada. He went through the room where the beds were, and he could see her lying there on the bed with her eyes shut. He didn't want to wake her up, so he tiptoed on into the kitchen and cleaned and cooked the chicken. He thought he would go crazy, smelling the meat while it was cooking, but he didn't touch a bite of it until it was done, and he poured some broth in a bowl and took it to Vada. He couldn't eat until he knew she wasn't hungry any more.

He stood by the bed with the steam coming up out of the rich yellow soup. She was still asleep, and he said, "Vada, Vada, wake up. I got you something to eat. Something good." But she didn't move, and he said, "Vada, Vada," again. She wouldn't wake up. He looked at her good, and then he knew. He had known she was dead when he went through the room the first time, but it just took him so long to really know it. That's the way he was. It took him a long time to really know things. He was like that about Mr. Landis. The thing that he was supposed to remember and to know about him, the thing that was so important for him to know, he couldn't really know. He had tried and tried, and he just couldn't. Someday he would. But right then he had to cry for Vada. He was the only one she had to cry for her, and his crying fell into the yellow soup, and he did not want the food any more.

Jed finally came home, and they buried her at the foot of the hill under the chinaberry tree. He cut out a wooden cross and put it at the head of the grave, and it was like she had never been.

After a while, he went down the road to the Landis' house. It was a big house, a big, ugly green house with gables and a wide porch on two sides. The folks were there, all kind of folks. The farmers were out in the yard, and the stranger folks were on the gallery.

He stood with the men, listening to the low talking and watching the brown tobacco juice and snuff splatter on the gray ground.

Mr. Ora said, "It's a bad way to die. Agin God."

Somebody else said, "I never woulda thought she'd a kilt herself. Not her."

"You can't tell about folks. How they're thinking, that is."

"You could always know what Mrs. Landis was thinking about. Money, money."

"Maybe that's what done it. Maybe she stopped thinking about money long enough to think what kind of woman she was, and then she just shot her brains out."

"Everybody can believe what he wants to, but myself, I believe there's more to it than meets the eye. What would she a wanted to kill herself for?"

"Thar you go trying to make something foul out of her dying. That's all you good for, to try to stir up some mess."

"I ain't no sech trying to stir up nothing. It don't make no never mind to me if'n she killed herself or if'n somebody else done it. She's cold stone dead. Ain't no arguing that."

"Yore right about that. She's shore nuf dead."

"You seen her?"

"Yep, I seen her, if'n you can call it a her. Leastways I seen the pieces."

"How come you get to see her? Thought they wasn't letting nobody in there to look at her."

"I was one of the first ones to get here, that's why. Fact is, I helped old man Landis and Mason get the pieces together and bring her in the house. God, I hope I don't never have to do nothing like that agin."

"Seems like a pity Mr. Landis had to do it. Musta been mighty hard on him seeing her like that and all."

"I wouldn't say so. If you ast me, he's bearing up pretty well."

"He's lived with her a long time."

"Yeah, maybe too long."

"Yeah, too long," he said. They looked at him with surprise on their faces. He looked at the ground, and they looked away again like he wasn't there.

"Could be he got tired of living with her maybe," a younger man said.

"You fool. Ain't you got no sense?"

"Shut up. Don't you let nobody hear you talking like that."

"Shut up," He said after the man, and they looked at him again.

Then the car with the radio aerial drove up, and the aerial quivered in the wind when the car stopped.

"Thar's the sheriff. Guess they is more to it than meets the eye."

"Didn't I tell you? Yawl too busy making somebody out a fool to listen to nothing. Reckon we'll find out who is the fools."

"Hush up, Ben. Can't you just hush up?"

The sheriff didn't look like any sheriff, to his way of thinking. He was a little dried up sort of fellow with glasses and no gun. He knew the man. He had seen him riding around with Mr. Landis, giving out little cards before he got to be the law. The sheriff went on into the house, and the talk started again.

"He ain't here on business. Him and Mr. Landis is friends."

"Why shore. That's it. He didn't even have no gun."

"That don't prove nothing. He don't never wear no gun."

"Well, just let me tell you something. I won't be surprised at anything he finds out. It jest ain't natural for a woman like Miz Landis to do away with herself. Anybody that loved a dime the way she did would be shore to cheat the devil outa his due as long as she could."

"Well, if'n she didn't do it, I'd be willing to shake hands with the one that did, myself." That was Harry Tripp. His baby had died because his wife was starving and couldn't give enough milk for it. Mrs. Landis was holding up their government rations until he paid a year-old bill at the store.

"Ain't no fittin' way to talk about the dead."

"Naw. It ain't fittin," he said, and watched them look at him from under their eyebrows. He turned around and walked up on the porch.

City folks, stranger folks in white shirts and ties and dresses that weren't cotton. Folks that stopped talking to look at him and then turn around and ask themselves questions. He squatted down against the wall and half closed his bad eye so that it wouldn't show too much and he listened.

A tall, skinny woman with little rat's teeth like Mrs. Landis's looked at him and then put up her fingers and talked through them to the man next to her. "Harvey, my God. He looks just like…" She drew her fingers together to stop the words and just looked at him.

"Dammit, Estelle, dammit." The man's voice was low and hard.

"I didn't think. But did you ever?" Her voice was lower, and he could feel her eyes keep running back to him.

A trembly old woman with brown splotches on her gray face stood next to them. "Poor Gladys, poor Gladys. To be buried without a face. To be buried with the coffin never being open so her loved ones can look upon her beloved face for a last time. Poor Gladys, poor Gladys."

"She's poor now, Mother, but she had plenty while she was alive," the man said. "I wonder how her money will be…"

"I can't get over that boy." The woman's eyes kept running back to him. She chewed fast on her gum, and her rat's teeth made it pop.

"Dammit, Estelle. I said dammit."

A tall boy with slick black hair walked up and propped against the gallery rail. "Who's the cropper with the wild eye?" he asked, jerking his head backward.

"It's obvious, isn't it?" the skinny woman said, sharp-like. She didn't sound surprised now. Just ugly.

All the while they were talking, he was listening and thinking, and the thought inside him that had waited all his life to be known, really known, was getting ready to be born. He could feel it bubbling down inside him, wanting to be remembered, creeping into the insides of his head. The talking was going on, and he could hear the words without even listening. It was about him. He knew that, and it didn't make him mad because they were saying that he looked like Mr. Landis. He felt nice all through this, especially inside his chest where it was growing big and big like a mountain, and in his head where the knowing was trying to be really knowing. And then the thinking stopped. He felt dead.

The woman was still talking, the red streaks from her neck pushing up into her flat face. "It's a disgrace. Just because Gladys couldn't have any children…"

And then his thought was back, so strong that he thought his head would burst with it. His stomach quivered, and the saliva got thick in his mouth. For he could remember, and the remembering brought the knowing he had lost in his blackness.

It was in the night, a long time ago, when his Pa was gone from home, and he had to get up to go outdoors. He was going behind the smokehouse, but he saw them, and he forgot to go. Mr. Landis was holding her hand, and in the moonlight she was so pretty and sad it made his heart hurt. "She knows, and she hates you and there's going to be trouble," he was telling her. "Now don't cry. It's the boy. If you would just send him to Harlow's, it would be all right. Then she wouldn't have to see him and be reminded. Just send him to Harlow's." And she was crying and saying no, no, no, no with her head going from side to side. Then Mr. Landis was shaking her and loving her in the shaking, and she was moaning about going away from all that hate, and he told her then she'd never go away from him, he'd kill her and himself first. He said it, and his saying it made everything go black. They were no more, not even specks or whispers in the darkness. He was alone and black with blackness, and a sad, strange wind rushed through him and carried him back to bed, and he went to sleep fast with the trembling black wind holding him tight.

It was a long time ago, but he could still remember that blackness. He had it until one day he looked at the gully behind the house, and it was deep. He looked at his long, long legs and looked all around and his Ma was gone. She had been gone a long time, and she never came back. His Pa never came back either, except one time, Jed said, and that was to take their sister Rhee away with him.

Sitting there on the porch with the kin woman's hard eyes running to and around him and the handkerchiefs wiping away sweat that pretended to be tears, he had become tired from the remembering of that night and from the knowing that he never could find all the remembering that would fill in that time of blackness. He stopped trying and listened to the sounds making like mourning around him.

Then Mr. Landis came out of the house with the sheriff. He didn't look any different, not like you'd think he'd look after raking the pieces of her together and smelling the ugly, rotten death of her. He had on the same clothes, the khaki britches and shirt that still had the dried splotches of blood and mud on them, and the black, greasy hat that he always wore pulled low to one side to shadow his eye a little. There was one thing though; he looked bigger and straighter, and the little puckers around his lips were loosened up.

Mr. Landis stood on the cracked concrete step with the sheriff saying, "Aye, God, Jim, I appreciate you coming, but don't you worry no more about it. Like I said, it was just her way. It being her time of life, you know, and I guess it just got too much for her. She ain't felt good for a long time. Even if'n it's agin the Good Book, I can't find it right of me or no living soul to cast no stones, now that she's gone. I swear I can't."

The sheriff's toe pushed the crack, and he didn't look up. "Naw, naw, can't nobody cast no stones, that's for sure. I'm mighty sorry, Henry, you know that. And if there's anything, anything at all I can do, just let me know."

Mr. Landis was not looking at the sheriff either now. He looked way off above the heads of the people toward where the treetops went into the sky, and you could tell he was seeing way off good and clear. "Well, Jim," he said, "I'm much obliged to you."

Then the sheriff was going through the crowd, and they were talking again, and some of them spoke to the lawman and some of them shook his hand. And Mr. Landis was going back into the house, saying to him the good words, the wanted words, "Hey, Boy, come in the house with me, boy."

And he did. Went right into the house behind him, right into the living room with the big flowered rug on the floor and the little lady chairs with the velvet seats and backs like he never would have done if she had been alive. They went on down the dark hall, past the death room where the women whispered around the bed where she lay, and on into the kitchen.

"Set down," he said, and they did.

For a long time Mr. Landis just looked at him. He felt the gaze down into the knowing part of him, the part that was thinking and he knew that Mr. Landis knew, even before he felt the shoe shove against his foot. The chicken blood was all mixed with dried mud.

"Why did you do it, boy?" He was not mad, or hurting, just seeing. That's what made Mr. Landis so big; he could see so good and know without doubting or wondering. "It don't make no difference now. None at all. But you had no reason, boy."

And then he told him all about it. And how the reason was in the ground back of his house, about how he had buried her wrapped in an old quilt, buried her hungry because there had been no funerals and no food and the rabbits could smell his hunger coming, and about the chicken soup being too late even before the shot had killed the chicken because Vada and he had been shot long ago by all the guns in the world. He told him about the blackness and the never knowing like other folks and the overwhelming hunger.

"I understand," Mr. Landis said. "I understand everything now." Then they looked at each other, and he thought the man's eye was the goodness and greatness of the eye of God.

Mr. Landis put a pan of water on the floor and gave him a rag. "Scrub your shoes now, boy." He scrubbed hard at the bloodstain, listening. "After the funeral, you'll come live with me. I won't have anybody then and you don't have anybody either. You never did have anybody. You'll have plenty to eat as long as I live; you won't ever be hungry again, and it don't matter about you not knowing things. It don't matter about that at all. Lots of times, the not knowing is better than the knowing. Believe me, boy, the not knowing is a blessing sometimes. I ought…"

He talked on and on, and the words wrapped him in warm

yellow, and he forgot the hungry days and Vada in the wood box under the ground and his Ma sitting on the ground crying in the night. And the knowing was not even important, after all. All he knew was that he belonged to the greatness and goodness of Mr. Landis now, and that was all he needed to know.

"You're hungry. Eat." Suddenly there was a big plate of meat and potatoes and bread on the table, and his stomach was hungry again and reached for the good taste. "That oughta be pretty good meat," Mr. Landis said. "It's a doe I killed yesterday over at the Coon Creek field. Didn't know it was a mama deer when I shot it, of course. Never shoot the mamas on purpose. Don't believe in it. But that ain't no reason to let the meat go to waste if you do shoot one by accident."

Mama deer. That's what Jed had said, once long ago. Mr. Landis' words brought back the echoes out of the blackness, and he could hear Jed saying over and over on that morning after the night of his Ma's crying in the yard: "It's just a deer I shot by accident, boy, and skinned in the night last night. But it's a mama deer, so it ain't no good to eat. A mama deer'll rot your insides out if'n you eat it. Hush now. Don't take on so, boy. Hush, I say. Ain't nothing but a mama deer. Ain't it, Rhee? Hush, now, before I swat you one. What you taking on so for, boy? Ain't I done told you it ain't nothing but a mama deer?" It hung upside down in the smokehouse, with the feet tied to the rafters, and it was slick and red from being skinned, and blood made a big dark wet spot on the ground under it.

"God damn him, God damn him," Rhee had said, and he said, "What?" and Jed fussed again. "Now you hush up too, Rhee, and take the boy in the house. Do like I say now. I'll take care of this deer. The boy ain't got no business looking at it. Nor you neither for that matter. Go on now."

And then he knew. With the deer meat taste in his mouth and the hungry walls of his stomach reaching up for the meat even as he swallowed it, he knew the thing about Mr. Landis he had been trying to remember all the long black and gray years. It wasn't a deer in the smokehouse on the morning after his Ma's crying in the night. It wasn't a deer at all.

He looked up at the man, and the goodness and the greatness of his clear eye was as black and wild as the bad eye. The man reached out and put his hand on his shoulder, and the inside of him was crying from the pain of knowing. And then his mind was running ahead of his legs, back, back hunting for the blackness of the unknowing that would stop the cold, hard hurting in him. He ran out of the big old house with the dead woman, past the silk and hair tonic of the city kin, past the overalled men with their spitting snuff and away from the wild black eye and the knowing.

The trees along the road he runs on are sometimes gray, but mostly they are black. Through the trees he can see the red slickness of the bleeding mama deer as it runs with him, racing through the black trees with him always toward the end of the road, to the big pit filled with the blessed blackness of unknowing and hunger.

THE POET'S DEER

THE Black Belt's July sun is always a prostitute: hot and gaudy and malignant. On a certain day of that summer of her in-betweenhood, its rays spread like a bright yellow fan across the girl's narrow virgin cot, soaking her in heat and heavy pre-waking dread. At first the dread was nameless; it floated about her associated only with the burnt orange of summer and the unpleasantness of facing a day of hot housework. A fly hummed across her face, skimmed the corner of her mouth, and made her jarringly awake. She opened her eyes, lay rigid and watched it settle with a tickle on her arm. She slapped viciously at the insect and grimaced when it sailed unhurriedly away. It had landed on the windowsill and was squatting in the sun, leering at her. She remembered then that she was going to hate this day especially because of the man who had come to visit.

He had arrived the night before just at bedtime. She had been in her darkened room, partially undressed, when she heard her uncle let him in. "Well, Ray Hawkins, you old son of a gun. Come on in, boy, come on in."

She heard a deep male voice reply and listened to the jovial blurring of their voices as she hurriedly redressed. She became nervous in her excitement, and the little corner of her soul that harbored an unsung song and a prayer without a god awoke and stirred hopefully. Around and around in her mind, like a musicless carousel, went her supplication, "Please let him be nice, please let something good happen, please, please." In the yellow-gray light from the kitchen she dug a smear of red from the impoverished lipstick tube with her little finger. She painted her mouth, then thoughtfully and cynically wiped it clean again. She listened. The man's voice was pitched too low for her to understand any words, but she liked the sound of it. Young, she thought, and strong and good. And her prayer, addressed to no one and to everyone who had ever longed, wound hurtingly around on the carousel platter inside her head. She did not beseech God. Once upon a time she had said, "God is great, God is good," with the consuming passion of her childhood's belief. That was when she had first come to live with her Uncle George and Aunt Edna after her mother's death. She had always said, "My holy Father," because then God seemed to belong to her in a personal way, the way no real father ever had. But she had overdone it.

She had begged with inarticulate abandon until the giver of all gifts wearied of her whining and spoke to her reproachfully in her sleep. "And what is it you want then, child? You know there is a Depression, and it won't last forever. Count your blessings. You may get tired of beans and fatback, but you don't go hungry. You have a roof over your head and relatives to care for you. Do you not have a Father who art in heaven? Now be quiet and say your prayers." She had been nine years old when she dreamed of being a nuisance to God. She had not bothered Him with her prayers since.

Then last night, sixteen years old and psychologically scarred by the last ten years of the Depression, she had stood in the dark and listened to male voices in an adjoining room. Like the desperate deer fleeing from savage dogs in Coffin's poem "Crystal Moment," her need to escape the ugliness of her life was as sharp as razor pain. She would not ask God for help. She was not nine years old, and although she still believed that God is great, she could not think Him good who allowed such misery to cripple a whole country. She pressed trembling hands to her sides and walked into the front room to meet the young, strong, and good voice.

She smiled when she saw him. The man thought it was for him, and he leered. He was not young, of course, or any of those other things; those who came to her uncle's house never were. She had not really thought it would be different.

"Hey, gal, I betcha don't know who this is."

"No, sir, I don't." She wished that she had not come out.

"Course she don't. My God, it's been ten years since I was down here, George."

The man was grinning a little under his thick, greasy mustache and watching her with squinting whiskey-red eyes. He was wearing a rumpled coffee-brown suit with a dingy tieless white shirt.

"That's the truth, ain't it," her uncle agreed.

"Fact is, George, I didn't even know you had any children, especially not a good-looker like this one." He leered again, and she stared in revulsion at the tight gray pinkness of his under lip.

Uncle George guffawed and slapped his knees. "Lord, man, we still ain't got no young'uns. You know, me and Edna don't gee-haw thataway. This here's Stella's girl Sissy. We took her to raise when Stella died. Been a while now, ain't it, gal?"

She nodded, listened to a discussion of the man's rank in the family as a distant cousin, the prosperity of his Blue Moon Café in a northern county, suffered through some more leers and remarks about her appearance and went to bed.

But on this, the next morning, waking and remembering, she was filled with a reluctance to begin the day. She put on a clean shirt, a pair of faded blue jean shorts and was lacing up her tennis shoes when her Aunt Edna came into the room.

"Who the hell is that in my bed?" she demanded of the girl, as she sat on the side of the cot to remove her oxfords and skin the stockings down legs corduroyed with the blueness of varicose veins.

"Ray Hawkins. He's a cousin from Tuscumb."

"Oh, lord, I won't get any sleep today. Reckon they stayed up all night drinking." She stepped out of her green waitress uniform, lay back on the cot and started a cigarette.

"I don't know. I went to bed," the girl answered. "Is he all right? I mean, except for drinking?" She did not look at her aunt but went to the mirror, pulling a comb through her tangled hair.

"What do you mean, all right?" Her aunt's voice had an antagonistic, after-being-up-all-night edge.

"I don't know. Does he behave?"

"How should I know how he behaves?" The aunt was garrulous now, propping up on one elbow. "What's the matter with you? I declare, Sissy, I don't know what I'm going to do with you. You don't have any friends of your own, and when I get a date for you, you're always worrying about how the boy'll behave." There were infinite versions of this familiar dialogue, and the girl tensed in anticipation. In disagreements with her aunt, she had always remained passive, somehow knowing with the wisdom of her aloneness, that she must never antagonize anyone.

"Look at me and answer when I talk to you," the aunt commanded.

At the cold hardness in her tone, the girl turned from the mirror. "I've never asked you to get me a date."

"No, that's just the trouble. If it was left up to you, you'd stick in this house till you rotted. Well, you've got to think about getting a husband." The cigarette ground out on the chipped iron bedstead.

"I don't want a husband. I want to go to school. You said I could. Besides, they're not boys. They're men, and I hate them, all of the men you send around here to paw me and blow their whiskey breath in my face. I'm tired of fighting them."

The heat was in the room like a blanket, and the tin top of the house seemed close enough to scorch her face.

"Well, if that's the way you feel about it, you'd better get your claws sharpened because T.J.'s coming tonight. Said to tell you he'd be here at eight o'clock."

The girl's eyes clouded. "T.J. Woods?"

"T.J. Woods?" the aunt mimicked in mock horror.

"But he's married."

"Oh, for heaven's sake. He's separated and practically divorced." She rolled over with her face toward the wall. "Now let me sleep."

"I won't. I won't go with him. You can't make me."

"Oh, damn. Stop taking on so. You can't afford religion."

"I can! You can't maybe, but I can. Why do you keep pushing men on me?" She could hear her voice shrill in the air, but she couldn't stop. "Sometimes I think you want me to get pregnant and have to marry so you won't have to use Mama's money to send me to college. Is that it? Is it?"

The woman stiffened visibly on the bed, but she did not reply.

The girl's words rushed on. "You're a hot one to shove men on me. Don't think I don't know why you work at night. How long has it been since you and Uncle George…"

Her aunt looked at her then. "If you say one more word, I'll slap your face crooked. I have to kiss the asses of stinking truck drivers at night, then I come home to God knows what kind of trash in my house, and now you give me a lot of sass. I won't have it, you hear. Now get out of here." And she turned resolutely back to the wall.

So the July day began — without dreams or hope of dreams, all racing hot in purples and yellows and red under a tin roof with a man's eyes following her from stove to table to ironing board to back porch. He was sitting at the kitchen table when she came in, grinning obscenely with his overheard knowledge of the nakedness in her life.

"Up at the Blue Moon 'bout now the cook's slinging breakfast orders around like nobody's business." The daylight did not improve his looks or lessen the evil in his leer.

Uncle George put his arm around her waist as he always did before strangers. "Just you wait till you put one of Sissy's biscuits in your mouth. She's a better cook any day than her Aunt

Edna."

So she made the biscuits while her uncle went to the barn, and the man slurped black coffee from a saucer as he watched her every movement.

"By God, I got a idea. You ought to come up to Tuscumb and work for me in the Blue Moon. I got one helluva place. You'd like it for sure."

"I'm going to school this fall."

"Zat so? What kind of school now? One of them business schools?"

"Oh, no, I'm going to college," she said aloofly, with an unmistakable trace of superiority in her voice. She yearned to be haughty and tell him he was a fool for thinking she was the common Blue Moon type of girl. But she only said, "Of course, I may go into nurse's training in Birmingham. That's what Aunt Edna wants me to do. Says it's more practical. Mama left enough money for my education."

She did not usually talk so much, but today she had to hide behind words — cool, casual, aloof words.

But she knew the man was not perceptive. He had spent too much of his life in the deceptiveness of blue lights at night, beer bottles, and coarse men and women. He was incapable of feeling clean kinship with her, and she would not beg him to understand her. They were pursued and pursuer, and she knew it. So she prolonged the safe, aloof talk to give her a head start. She was running miles ahead of him, but she was tired already, and the sun was not nearly so hot as it would get.

He insisted on helping her gather dinner vegetables while her uncle went to the cow pasture. They hovered over a row of butter beans, one on each side, squatting and rising, pulling at the few shriveled beans, feeling the skin-reddening sear of the sun from above and the cracked, dry dirt beneath their feet, his hands grabbing at hers from time to time, always to the accompaniment of stupid, middle-aged flirtation.

His amorous intentions for the moment came to a climax as

he followed her up the wooden porch steps.

"Wait a minute," he said, directly behind her.

She turned. "What is it?"

And because she had not expected it, at least not so soon, when she thought she was still safely ahead of him, she could not move when he reached his hands toward her bare legs.

"Put your legs together," he said and she obeyed mechanically.

"Why?"

"I just want to see something. Uh huh. Look here. You need to fill out your legs right in here." And his hands were running down the insides of her legs, emphasizing a small space where they did not meet when she stood straight. His hands stroked and darted near the edge of her shorts. She shivered, hard goose bumps of fear and distaste washing from her shoulders down her body in waves, but she could not act. She only said, "Don't do that now."

A hint of her young fury reached him. He grinned. "Don't get mad now, Sissy. I was just making a suggestion." He followed her into the kitchen. "A girl like you ought to take advantage of all she's got. I wouldn't be fresh with you. Innerested in all my kinfolks and like to help all I can."

She sat down with the pan of beans between her legs to shell as she usually did, then hastily pulled the pan onto her lap.

"Well, I don't really need any help."

"Sounded like you needed a little help the way you and your Aunt Edna was carrying on in there this morning," he said slyly.

"Aunt Edna and I will work things out," she replied curtly.

"O.K., but you just remember I'm always ready to take care of you if'n you'll come up to the Blue Moon. You jest remember that, you hear."

"All right. But I don't—"

"What y'all yapping 'bout?" Her uncle came in, smelling of manure. "You must have a way with women, boy, to get that Sissy talking."

And then they were gone in the car. To the liquor store, she felt sure. She wondered how far ahead she was now. Had she ever been ahead since coming to this house? She knew that there existed a higher plain that her mother used to sing about, sweetly and sincerely. She knew it because she felt the need of its existence in her hurtingly tight chest, but she did not know if there was a road to it from where she was.

Her fingernails ached from prying open the tough bean hulls. "I'm pressing on the upward way. New heights I'm gaining every day. Lord, plant my feet on higher ground." The words of the old hymn whispered through her mind, trailing remembrances of her mother, but bringing no golden images of God or church to comfort her. "Lord, lift me up," up, up, up above scratched oilcloth table covers, naked light bulbs, fly-specked ceilings, linoleum floors, cane-bottom chairs, young guitar-twanging relatives with dump-truck coloring, above impossibly bad grammar and manners, above, just above. Above the abject terror of a ten-year-old girl with a newly dead mother on a night when forced, because of company, to sleep between a strange and unsympathetic uncle and aunt. Above the nightmarishness of waking to find oneself clasped tightly to the body of a stinking, union-suited old man, of suffering his half-drunken, half-sleeping pressing, of crying to the aunt, please change places with me, please. Suffering the laughing why, insisting I just can't sleep in the middle, please Aunt Edna. Then the query is Uncle George loving you? Yes, yes I'm scared. Well, hush, don't wake everybody up. George, George, turn over and stop snoring. He's asleep. He thought he was hugging me. Hush now. Go back to sleep. Just above, a higher plain.

When she had finished the cooking, and the men had not returned, she decided to shower off her heat in the little makeshift bath on the back porch. Gratefully, she felt the hard water on her hot body. She felt like crooking her finger childishly and saying goody-goody to the sun, now ominously making the tin above her head creak and pop. Her respite was short-lived. As she turned the water off and reached for a towel, the plastic curtain jerked aside and the man's eyes widened at her nakedness.

"Woops," he said, letting the curtain fall. "Didn't know you were in there, Sissy. Sorry as hell."

Sorry as hell, he said, but she could feel his presence on the other side of the curtain, unmoving, waiting. Her body, even its softest parts, turned bumpy and hard with the only kind of coldness possible under the July sun. Her real hatred began then. She put it on as she dressed, like a red winter mitten stretched tightly over her heart.

She walked by him, seeing only the stretching of the thin pink lips under the mustache. His whiskey odor floated menacingly around him, a reminder that he was gaining on her, that the race was quickening. But she was still ahead, pressing on the upward way to a higher plain.

She went to the front room, ran her hands over the cracked blackness of the old upright piano that had been her mother's. The music called time out and liberated her, and she raced ahead of the hound. The sounds of music buoyed her with the sweet affirmation of the magic of romantic love blossoming in the light of moonbeams. That the moon would reveal the face of her true love, as the lyrics promised, was a seductive fancy that fed her yearning, her longing for love. But juxtaposed to the joy expressed in the lyrics was the haunting sound of the music that made her inexpressively sad at the potential for heartbreak.

At the sound of a brisk knock on the screen door, she reluctantly ended the music to reenter the reality of her wasteland environment.

"Hello, Sissy. Are we on time for dinner?"

She relaxed and felt almost joyous. She always welcomed the cheerfulness, the sincerity of the Mormon missionary who came occasionally to remind her uncle that he had inherited his father's religion and ought to pay more respect to Joseph Smith's teachings.

"Come in, Elder Jason. I was just to going to set the table."

She was acutely aware of the missionary's companion, a tall young man impeccably dressed in a light gray suit and trying hard to appear very proper and serious as befits a Mormon on his first mission. The soft gray hat almost shadowed a deep dimple in his chin.

While Elder Jason, relaxed and genial as always, introduced them, the girl was embarrassedly conscious of her bare brown legs and disconcerted by the physical attractiveness of the young man as he pushed his hat back and smiled at her. Suddenly standing in the shabby room, with the gaudy plastic curtains and the artificial flowers, the good, clean, strong voice had a face and a tall body and a white shirt without stains. God is great, God is good; the refrain from her early childhood's blessings began to stir in her.

"You play 'Clair de Lune' with a lot of passion," Elder Hanes said.

She knew that he was perhaps wondering at her playing it at all, but she did not try to explain. "Well, it's sort of special."

"Like Joseph Smith?" He was smiling.

"A little like Joseph Smith, I think." And she was smiling, too, as a little breeze eased timidly through the room. She could hardly restrain herself. She felt like throwing up her arms and dancing wildly around the room. Her gratitude flowed out to Joseph Smith, who was not so busy with the sick and hungry that he could not send a missionary to help the poet's deer. Throughout the dinner she sang inside herself.

The cousin was very drunk. He ate an enormous meal, cramming the food in a noisy way through the obscene grin that had become permanent. He never took his eyes off the girl, and he did not talk.

Dinner over, the family sat in the front room and talked with the missionaries until Elder Jason announced, "Well, we're certainly enjoying this, but we've quite a few other calls to make this afternoon."

Uncle George was immediate hospitality. "Oh, don't hurry

off now. You know we always expect you to spend the night with us."

"Well, we'll certainly take you up on that if it's not too much trouble. I've stayed with you so much on my trips to Mason that I feel right at home here."

"We'll look for you at supper then," Uncle George said, shaking hands very cordially.

Elder Hanes was looking at her, his hat twirling in his hands. "The dinner was delicious. I hope you'll play some more for us tonight."

"Yes," she said. "I will."

"That's a promise. We'll be back."

And they were gone, leaving her again racing blindly into the sun. Her breath caught, and her eyes smarted from the hot stillness of the air. The man was behind her, in front of her, by her side, always with the odor of him choking her.

She worked busily at the sink. He touched her shoulder. "Ya been thinking any 'bout coming up to the Blue Moon wid me, huh? I got an idea. Jest pack up yore clothes and les us high tail it out of here tonight. What cha say, Sissy girl? My wife, she'll take good care of you. Why, we just need a little girl like you to pet. I got plenty of money. Rake it in at the Blue Moon. I'd get you some purty dresses and keep your pockets full of nickels to play the Rockola with. How's that sound to you, huh?"

She put the dishes up, rattling them noisily. "No, I can't go," she said, and the whiskey smell was coming over her shoulder. When she turned around, he was so close she could not move to get around him.

"Sumpin been bothering me all day. It's what color yore eyes are. Be still now." He took her chin in his hand. "Lemme look good," and peering into her face he kissed her before she could believe he would attempt it.

"There's a nice little smooch for my pretty lil blue-eyed cousin."

She pushed against him. "Leave me alone," she gasped. She

didn't know what to do then; she couldn't fight him. She ran to the outdoor toilet; he followed and waited until she came out. She started to the neighbor's, but he went, too. So she turned around and came home, always jerking out of his reach. She couldn't stay in the house. It was gaspingly hot and his hands caught at her constantly. She went out into the lean-to where her uncle was mending shoes for a Negro. The man and his two grown sons squatted on the ground and talked. She sat in a yard chair and listened to the soft thumping sound of the tacks being driven into rubber. The cousin sat on the arm of the chair, his buttocks shoving against her and his hand going across her shoulder. She cringed and slid down on the ground near her uncle. He followed her quickly, placing himself close beside her.

"Yes, sir, George, you got one fine little niece here. She's a real good-looker if I ever saw one. Been trying to get her to come work for me at the Blue Moon." He put his hand on her leg. The Negro boys looked at each other and back at them, but their old father looked off into the distance.

Her Uncle George didn't pay her any attention. His eyes and mind seemed riveted on the job before him, his mouth working in that odd way he had when concentrating. She eased closer to her uncle and tried to make him notice her dilemma, but he saw only the tacks and his thumb.

The day wore on in its heat. She couldn't find any respite in any of the rooms because none of them had locks. Finally, she set up the ironing board in the hot kitchen, faced him, and said, "Listen, I'm tired of running from you. You're a dirty, drunk old man and I'm sick of you. You can tell Uncle George if you want to. But if you touch me one more time, I'm going to smash this hot iron in your face." Then, she cried. The tears washed down her face and sizzled on the upraised iron.

He misinterpreted the tears for weak resolve. "Oh, now Sissy girl, this here's yore cousin Raymond you talking to."

Her eyes were bright from the tears and the day's hating. "I said stay clear away from me," she said, her voice and eyes hard and the iron upraised.

He backed away and looked at her. She began ironing a shirt, and he started toward her again. But when she stared at him unwaveringly, he turned and went out into the yard.

A little later Uncle George came in to tell her to fix supper for the elders but not for Raymond. He'd decided to go on over to his brother's in Cedar Hills.

When she put up the ironing board, it was cooler. She went outside and tried to hold the dusky darkness in her arms. God is great, God is good, her mind chanted, and her heart laughed.

She cooked quickly and then showered. She was clean and cool in a pink voile dress, and the kitchen looked brighter with a white tablecloth and the tall tea glasses.

"I'm getting hungry now. Wish they'd come on," Uncle George complained.

"They'll come before long," she assured him. The young missionary had said, "That's a promise. We'll be back."

When they had not returned at 7:30, she urged her uncle to go ahead and eat. "You eat. I'll wait and eat with them."

She went into the front room and began to play the piano. She would like to be playing when he came. A little after eight o'clock, she heard a car drive up. She heard it above the piano because she was anticipating it, but she did not stop playing. She was a little nervous, but very happy. She played louder so that she could pretend she did not hear the screen door open. It would be nice if it were just him alone without Elder Jason, and he would lean over and put his cheek against hers and say, "Oh, my love, you don't have to be sad anymore." It would be so nice.

A face leaned over her shoulder, and a sickening cologne and hair tonic odor assailed her. "Hiya, pretty baby." It was T.J. Woods, separated and almost divorced.

Trapped, she experienced a demonic epiphany: She had no chance because there were too many hounds closing in on her.

In the car, en route to a notorious local honky-tonk, she felt her heart lurch when she recognized a passing car carrying the young missionary to keep a promise to the poet's deer.

Would he be disappointed, she wondered, now quiescent, resigned, listening to the baying of the dogs rushing madly at her in the hot July night.

God is great. God is good.

Bless Her Heart

When Maggie Evans entered a room, people noticed, not because she was important but because she was attractive and stylish. Youth and beauty were rare qualities in people at the Cahaba Nursing Home, so attention perked up when she walked through the common area and headed for her grandmother's room. The R.N. at the desk gave her a friendly nod and smiled at the skinny jeans, turquoise top with its fashionable twist at the point of cleavage, and the stiletto heels that clicked smartly on the tiled floor.

At the entrance to the hall of Wing B, Maggie drew a deep breath and looked at the old and ill residents parked in wheelchairs on both sides of the hall. When an ancient black man with a huge drooping and drooling underlip reached out to touch her, she smiled at him and continued to walk, soothing a tiny hump-backed woman crying desperately that she needed to pee, plumping up another who was about to slide out of her chair, and retrieving a book from the floor for a little gnome of a man. The features of all reminded her of cruel caricatures, and she couldn't help thinking of what lay ahead in her own old age.

But today she was focused on a mission to gather information and hoped that her grandmother would be helpful. Often, the one-hundred-year-old would be totally uncooperative. Her condition was called senile dementia.

Maggie entered Room 129 to a familiar scene. Two old women, one noticeably younger than the other, lay in side-by-side single beds, her grandmother in grumpy disarray, her mass of beauty-parlor white hair framing a gaunt face with bluish pouches under her eyes, the other woman in total stillness, lying rigidly on her back under white unrumpled sheets, eyes closed and arms folded across her chest in a casket pose. As always, Maggie gently patted the arm of the stroke victim and then sank down in the recliner between the two beds, facing her grandmother, whom she did not touch, having learned in her childhood that her grandmother disliked hugs.

"How are you, Granny?" she asked, to get a feel for the mood of the day.

The old woman's answer made it clear. "Well, I'm a hundred years old. How do you think I feel?"

Maggie tried teasing. "Well, getting to be that old ought to make you feel like celebrating."

"I do celebrate — every time the laxative works or I find my dentures in the commode." To underscore her sarcasm, she pushed her dentures forward and clicked them at her.

"Well, I'm glad you still have a sense of humor, Granny."

But Maggie was impatient with small talk today. "I hope you're up to helping with a school project," she said.

The old eyes, bright and as lucid as Maggie had seen them in a long time, showed no interest. "I figured you wanted something or you wouldn't have come."

"Now, you know I come when I can. I'm in graduate school and have classes all week. That's what I need your help with."

"If I remember right, you are getting a doctoral degree. And somebody with a grammar school education is supposed to help you with your summa cum laude business?" Maggie knew that using the Latin term was her way of denigrating her granddaughter's academic aspirations.

"I'm at the stage where I have to choose a subject to write my dissertation on," Maggie explained. "It's history, you remember."

"I was never any good at history — all those dates and wars and countries."

"But you don't have to know history. I just want you to tell me what you remember about your life during the Great Depression. My dissertation professors are encouraging me to focus on a particular aspect of that era of history, and I thought your memories might help me to settle on something definite." She realized that she was vague. What did she hope to get from her interviewee with such a lame preamble?

But she reckoned without the old woman's need to talk, to communicate with someone who really wanted to hear what she had to say. Perhaps she, Faith Baldwin, could tell the story of her life and validate those hundred years. So she launched off on a monologue that would take Maggie into the enigma of a heart of darkness that flourished during the Depression in the Alabama Black Belt.

"You may not know it, because your mama didn't believe it and wouldn't have told you, but you are descended from Old South aristocracy." And she met Maggie's stare straight-on as if daring her to dispute it. As a matter of fact, Maggie had heard the story as a child and did not believe it. But she didn't mind if Granny played fast and loose with the truth. "My mother," the old woman resumed, "was the niece of Jefferson Davis."

Maggie pretended surprise to encourage her. "The President of the Confederacy?"

"That's right. After the war, the Davis family got scattered. Mother's family came through Alabama on their way to Georgia. They camped beside a creek in Rabbit Run in the southeast of Cahaba County, and mother and her brother decided to take their possessions and remain there to farm. Life was hard on women at that time, and farm women had to work in the fields. My mother was plowing one day when a man on a horse stopped and watched her. She couldn't get the plow turned around at the end of a row of cotton. The man got off his horse, took the reins from her and turned the plow.

"If I heard mother say it once, I heard it a hundred times: 'If you'll marry me, you'll never have to plow again,' the man told her. That man was my daddy, and he was as good as his word. He was hard-working and frugal, and women in his family did not work in the fields. Mother hammered it into me: 'When you marry, have it understood that you will not work in the fields; remember that you're a lady.'"

And the pride in her voice was evident as she recalled her family's connection to a distinguished family and her mother's insistence on a lady's role. As if reminded by the reference to being a lady, she asked Maggie to hand her the bottle of Lubriderm on the dresser. Concentrating on massaging the lotion onto her hands and withered arms, she paused. Concerned that she might get distracted, Maggie jump-started her, "And did you have it understood with Granddaddy?"

"Have what understood?" she asked, clearly groping for the way back into her story.

"You know, about not working in the fields." Maggie was not prepared for the malignant bitterness that infected her grandmother's speech when she resumed.

"There was an understanding all right. Fred Baldwin agreed, and I trusted him. Everybody knew him for a good, decent man who took care of his family. Owned a saw mill and made a good living. But everything changed when the Depression hit."

Maggie listened intently. This was what she wanted to hear. "Tell me more about Granddaddy Fred. Was he handsome?"

Anger seeped into her reply. "Too handsome. Tall, broad through the shoulders, sandy hair that looked like fire in the sunlight and brown eyes that could look right through you."

"But you were happy, weren't you?" Maggie prompted.

"Happy? I never got a chance to be happy. Right off the bat, your granddaddy gave me to understand that he'd be sharing income from the mill with his mother and his four younger brothers. And that wasn't all. Every time he bought something for me, he got something nicer for his mother. What did she know about nice things? She bragged about being a beauty when she was young, but I knew she was white trash. Served her right when Fred's daddy left her. Just disappeared one day. Folks suspected foul play until they realized a black woman on his place went missing at the same time. It wasn't hard to put two and two together."

She paused and blinked the watery, red-rimmed eyes that had long since lost all trace of lashes. "Do you hear me, Maggie girl? I'm talking about your great-grandparents."

"I hear you, Granny." Maggie said, bracing herself when one of the black workers entered the room. "But let's stop and take your medicine now." She smiled at the young LPN holding out a little cup of pills. Neatly dressed in pink scrubs that complemented her milk chocolate skin, the girl remained silent. Maggie suspected that she'd overheard Granny's remark.

"You don't have to shush me or change the subject," the old woman said. "Precious here knows how I feel about niggers. I told her when she first came to work here that we'd get along fine if she remembered her place and treated me like a lady. I don't have any patience with all this pretending to be equal." She grew peevish and reached for the medicine. "Where's the water?" she demanded, looking about her as if disoriented. With the ritual of medicine-taking complete, she reached out a claw-like hand to grasp the girl's arm. "You ain't mad at me, are you, Precious? You know I'm just an old fool. Don't pay me no mind, you hear?"

The girl left without a word.

Waiting a discreet minute to be sure the worker was out of earshot, Granny lowered her voice to confide, "You have to be careful here. If you do or say anything they don't like, they'll take it out on you." She moved the bed covers and pointed to her leg, which was bandaged halfway between her ankle and knee. "You see that?"

Maggie was concerned. "What happened?"

"The man that put me in the wheelchair dropped me and scraped a big flap of skin off the bone."

"Do you think it was intentional?"

"I don't think it. I know it. He was paying me back for scolding him because he was rude. You're just a victim here." There was a tone of cold acceptance in the words, as if she'd come to terms with her old age, ill health, and consignment to the purgatory of a nursing home.

Maggie had little patience with her grandmother's lady obsession, but she knew it was not all affectation, that she truly had the instincts of a lady.

Maggie returned to her mission. "Can we get back to the story now? You were telling me about the miscegenation in the family's background."

"Miscegenation? What's that?" The old eyes glittered.

"Sexual relations between people of different races."

"That's a mighty big word for something so low-down. The very idea makes me want to throw up." She moved her leg gingerly back under the cover with a fleeting look of pain. "Well, your great-granddaddy was never heard from again, and Fred took over the mill and ran it with the help of his brothers. We got married, built a nice little house, and saved some money. But the most important thing that happened in those early years was the birth of your uncle Bert. He was a perfect baby, and, looking back, I think it may have been a sin for me to love him so much."

She closed her eyes as if to shut out the present and retreat to the past to remember. "He was a pure joy. Had his father's laughing brown eyes and my daddy's sweet temper. From the time he was a baby he drew people like a magnet. Everyone wanted to touch him. Like they were trying to absorb some of the happiness that seemed to warp around him like a rainbow. I told Fred that I didn't want any more children, but when Bert was two years old, Fred put the baby out of our bed and took me against my will. And what that got me was your mother."

From this point on, it was clear that the old woman had entered a place where hatred took over. Her audience was irrelevant. It mattered only that she give voice to the bitterness harbored in her heart for a lifetime.

"I never really loved her. I hated her even in the womb." The words crawled out of her mouth like a viper.

The stark, unashamed admission caused Maggie's heart to leap. She wanted to cry out to the old woman to stop, not to say such hurtful words. She looked at the countenance of the woman in the other bed, wanting to say, "Don't listen. She doesn't mean it."

But the narrative continued. "I was sick as a dog for nine whole months carrying her. Then I tore so bad during the delivery that I was never the same. Fred, bless his black heart, complained that his pleasure was diminished. I tried to love her, and I never neglected her. People always said Bert was my child and Dreena was Fred's child. He doted on her and refused to let me punish her. Like that time when she kept pulling her dress up and wouldn't obey me when I told her to stop. I got a switch and gave her a couple of licks, but he jerked the switch away from me and laid the law down that I was never to hit her again. When I tried to tell him that I just wanted her to grow up to be a lady, he stormed out at me that he already had one lady too many in his house."

She paused as if not knowing where to go next with her story. Finally, she said, "Well, the children grew up. When Bert was sixteen and Dreena fourteen, the Depression came and everything changed. Work at the mill dried up. Nobody had money to buy lumber. We did what everybody else did; we leased some land and started farming. We moved in with Fred's mother and three brothers that were still single and managed to get through that first year after the stock market crashed on our savings. But the money was gone before we knew it, what with feeding four grown men three meals a day with no income. I thought my life was hard, cooking and washing, and cleaning for that bunch of men and caring for a bitching mother-in-law."

"But bless your heart, it got worse. When I complained about the cost of feeding the brothers, they moved away in the middle of growing season, and Fred was left with a farm too big for him to handle. I will remember until my dying day when he told me that Bert and I would have to work with him in the fields. When I reminded him of his promise, he told me that I could go back to being a lady if we survived the Depression. He wouldn't hear of Dreena going to the fields. She was too young and would do the cooking, he said.

"Bert was eager to do a man's work and got his daddy to let him plow. A tall, strong boy, he caught on quickly, handling the plow and mule with confidence. One day Fred sent him to a two-acre new ground where he wanted to plant velvet beans for cattle feed. I told him not to send Bert there because it was dangerous, what with the stumps and tangled growth and all. But he wouldn't pay me no mind. Said he wouldn't have his son tied to his mother's apron strings any longer. To reassure me, he reminded me that he always carried his pistol to shoot snakes or kill a rabbit if we were lucky enough to come across one.

"On that day, he and I went to hoe in a field adjoining the new ground where we could keep an eye on Bert. We watched him hitch old Jim to the plow and carefully wrap the reins around both wrists, as his daddy had taught him, to have better control of the mule. He plowed one row, looked up at us and waved as he turned the plow around. I thought he would be all right then and tried to hoe faster to catch up with Fred, who was half a row ahead of me.

"It was hot as blazes, and I stopped to wipe sweat off my face. In that instant I heard a loud cry of 'Whoa, whoa,' and looked to see the mule spooked by a horde of hornets nesting in a clump of brush disturbed by the plow. The animal went crazy from the stings and bolted out of control. My beautiful boy was dragged to death. He couldn't free himself from the reins, and he was dead by the time Fred could shoot and kill the mule."

The voice stopped, and Maggie could believe that her grandmother's life had, in a way, stopped with the tragedy of her cherished son's death. But before her emotions could generate any pity, the voice continued, strong and coherent and a little insane.

"Is that enough Depression for you?" She squinted at Maggie

with malicious eyes. "I've got more," she threatened.

"Surely nothing else could be so terrible as that," Maggie said, totally unprepared for what followed.

"Well, you be the judge, Miss summa cum laude," she said, her voice curling in sarcasm. When Maggie did not respond, she plunged ahead. "Fred carried him home in his arms, stumbling across the field, trampling the corn stalks, staggering up the porch steps and laying him out on the long kitchen table. He was unrecognizable as a human being. The rough ground had chewed up his skin and the sharp blade of the plow had done its devil work, mutilating the body that had been so perfect. The dragging had shredded his clothes, and when I tried to cut them off, I couldn't.

"I just sat down and looked at him. Fred was no help. He left for the sawmill where he would make the coffin."

"It was left to me to get my child ready for burial. I couldn't do it. I wouldn't do it. I didn't have to. There was Dreena, alive and bawling over her dead brother. I hated her for being alive while he lay a corpse. I remember slapping her, and that slowed the tears long enough for me to make her understand she had to wash him and dress him for eternity. I forced myself to watch her do it. At first, she shrank from touching the body, and her hands trembled when she squeezed out the bloody wash cloth. But I felt no pity for her. Hatred was alive in my soul; it was like the sour taste of vomit in my mouth. The blistering day inched on, and I sat under that hot tin roof, fighting the fumes of blood and death. Near the end of the bathing, something strange happened. The bathing strokes became loving and gentle, and I knew that she had come to terms with the death." She became silent, and Maggie wondered if she had talked herself out.

But she resumed. "Folks nowadays talk a lot about closure. Dreena got closure and remained sweet. God, she was sickeningly sweet. But there was no closure for me. My depression was fueled by hatred and so the Great Depression lasted for half a century for me. Everybody loved my daughter except me. And I just couldn't."

When the voice ceased, the room seemed pregnant with a sudden silence. Reeling from the emotional confession she had been subjected to, Maggie was startled to hear a muffled sound from the other bed. The occupant of the bed, who had been comatose for two years, stirred, and one of the arms which had been so decorously folded across the chest dangled over the side of the bed. But it was the face which riveted Maggie's gaze. It was alive with a glow of pink-cheeked sweetness, and the clear blue eyes were awash with tears. Maggie's mother had come back from the living dead to suffer again the ultimate hurt of being an outcast from a mother's heart.

After experiencing the shock and jubilation of her mother's revival, Maggie wanted revenge for her mother's hurt and thought fleetingly of grasping the old woman's bandaged wound and crushing it for the exquisite pain it would cause. But she rejected the urge, seeing that lucidity had vacated the old eyes, had prowled back into the blankness of dementia.

The Legacy

Rube Burrows. It was a common enough name, but to Jeremy it was a poem of a name, with whispers of history, romance, and magic in it. He had known the name, almost from the cradle, as had everyone else in Linden. The bearer of the name, now moldering in a graveyard in Lamar County in northwestern Alabama, was a bona fide outlaw. His flamboyant capture and death in Marengo County became Linden's claim to fame. The town fathers had wasted no time after Rube's death in immortalizing the train-robbing legend. With a lot of grunting and a little cursing, the men had installed the impressive inscribed stone marker on the lawn in front of the old courthouse, each one silently proud of owning a rare piece of history.

One of the first things Jeremy learned to read was the inscription on Rube's marker. Bored with the "See Dick run" books used in school to teach reading, he took his elementary knowledge of consonants and vowels to the marker and, with Herculean mental energy, deciphered the words and thrilled to their meaning. Upset that the uncut Bermuda grass was obscuring the last line of the inscription, he tore at the offending grass, yanking it out of the ground with six-year-old fury. Finished, he took off his worn red shirt and wiped the monument clean of dirt and grass. That was the first overt manifestation of his idolatry. Without knowing it, he had sold his soul for the sake of a story with his father unintentionally brokering the deal.

The saga of Jeremy's flirtation with dark fantasy began innocently enough with a casual question for his father as they sat on the porch of their home, battling the heat of the August sun.

"Poppa?" the child asked lazily, pushing with his feet to keep the swing in motion.

"Yeah , Son?" His father's chair rocked in concert with the swing.

"Can you tell me about the man on the marker over there at the courthouse?"

He thrust his hand toward the fabled old building dominating the landscape across the street. It looked majestic, its three massive two-story columns gleaming whitely in the last splashes of sunlight. Built in 1848 to serve as the seat of Marengo's county government, it was an imposing structure, with the downstairs partitioned into several rooms and a pair of great exterior stairs circling up to a huge auditorium where court was held. Originally, a crude wooden building was built behind the courthouse to serve as a jail. Though the business district of the town shifted several blocks southward and a new jail and courthouse were built, the grand building in Old Town remained as a proud reminder of antebellum architecture. Jeremy's father, Durwood Upchurch, considered it a part of his legacy, descending, as he did, from Old South plantation aristocracy. And now, with a malicious depression nibbling away at the stability, codes, and culture of a remnant of the old order, he wondered what kind of legacy he would leave his child. The Great Depression, he thought cynically, would have something to say about that.

This child was only six years old, but he was already questioning, hunting something to counter the stultifying effects of a world of want.

Now here he was, wanting to know who Rube Burrows was. Durwood peered into the creeping darkness. "Well, son, which Rube Burrows do you want to know about?" A born storyteller, he enjoyed creating suspense.

"I didn't know there was more than one."

"Actually, there were two. You want to hear about the historical Rube Burrows, the facts of his life and death as recorded in historical records, or the Rube Burrows and his adventures as created in stories that people made up?"

"I want to hear about both — about everything." He leaned forward, forgetting to swing.

"It makes sense to consider the real Rube first. There is proof positive that he was born and raised in Lamar County, that his parents were Allen and Martha Burrows, who made their living by farming, that he was a cowboy on his uncle's ranch in Texas for many years and then owned his own ranch. He worked occasionally for the railroad. All of that biographical detail is documented, so we know it's true." He slapped at a mosquito whining relentlessly around his ear. "For four years, from 1886 to 1890, he led a life of crime, robbing trains mostly, that made him an infamous fugitive."

"What's infamous, Poppa?"

"It means being famous for bad things."

"And a fugitive is someone who's running from the law. Right?"

"Right. It was a long run for Rube, with law enforcement and dozens of railroad detectives on his trail. Time and time again they almost caught him, only to have him outwit them and escape, his gloating laughter lingering behind him. In four years and in four states, he robbed eight passenger trains."

"What states, Poppa? Alabama?"

"Yep. He held up one train in our state, two in Mississippi, one in Arkansas, and four in Texas."

"Did he get a lot of money?" His voice registered an uncommon interest, a fact noted by his father.

"I've heard it estimated at about $20,000."

"Man, oh man, that would buy a lot of marbles and peppermint sticks." And in Jeremy's mind, a platoon of red and white candy sticks bowed and paraded with a regiment of slick, gaudy marbles.

"Getting low on marbles, Bud?"

"Yes, Sir. Just got ole Rusty left. And he don't thump too

good 'cause he's chipped on one side."

"Think he'll hold out till the Depression is over?"

"I ain't got much hope."

"Don't say 'ain't,' Jeremy," his mother said from her rocking chair on the darkened end of the porch. "Civilized people don't use a depression as an excuse to debase language."

"Then I guess you couldn't use hard times as an excuse to rob trains, could you?"

His father answered, saying the morally correct thing, though it pained him. "Nope. Reckon not."

"Not even if somebody robbed the train to give to the poor?"

"You mean, like Robin Hood?"

"Yes, Sir. Robin Hood was a hero, wasn't he?"

"That's what they say. And some folks even said Rube was a Robin Hood." The tone of wistfulness in his voice suggested that he himself might be one of those folks.

There was a loud, emphatic cough from the other end of the porch. But Jeremy was not deterred and prompted his father back into the Rube story. "What did he look like, Poppa?"

And Durwood Upchurch, a short man with a lumpish physique, prematurely balding, and squinting through thick rimless glasses, described his alter ego.

"I saw a wanted poster one time, put up by the Pinkerton National Detective Agency. It offered a $700 reward for the capture of Reuben Houston Burrows after he robbed the Southern Express Company of $3,500. That was the St. Louis, Arkansas, and Texas Railroad. The poster gave a detailed description of Rube. Said he was thirty-two years old, six feet tall, and weighed about 160 pounds. Had blue eyes. Said he had this blonde mustache and used Hair Vigor to darken his sandy-colored hair. Left arm was a little shorter than his right one, and he had a lounging gait, usually with his hands in his pockets. Partial to dark clothes and woolen shirts. Wore a size eight boot."

"What about his gun, Poppa? Bet he was a good shooter, huh?" Durwood paused and watched the sun, now like a gaudy egg yoke, inch into the horizon. He allowed himself to join the child and slide into the imaginary world of little boys captivated by the exciting heroics of the old West and its larger-than-life cowboys. "When Rube rode, he had his rifle in a scabbard, and he carried a forty-five caliber gun in a low-slung holster. Good shot. But never killed a man in a train robbery."

Robbed of the killer image, Jeremy was only slightly disappointed. "No killing?" he asked, wanting to be sure. "But that's a good thing," he assured himself.

"Nope," Durwood said, choosing not to reveal that the train robber was reported to have killed a man in north Alabama in a violent rage. "For the most part, a decent man." He was conscious of the agitated rocking of his wife's chair, the rockers slapping the wooden boards of the porch viciously. But he plunged ahead, refusing to be intimidated by the disapproval littering the air around them. "Smart, too," he dared to throw in the direction of the offended chair.

"Smart how, Poppa?"

"Well, just think of his modus operandi. Once he decided to be a robber, he planned carefully. Before that first robbery, he went into the little town of Bellevue in Texas, not too far from his ranch. At the depot, he checked the train schedule and then scouted out the nearby woods for a meeting place for himself and his two fellow robbers." He warmed to the excitement generated by his imagination. "But the genius of his plan was that he and his cohorts lay in wait for the train when it stopped on the outskirts of the town to fill up at the water tank."

Jeremy was restless. "How come that was genius, Poppa?"

"Well, the genius part was that when the train stopped there, the passenger coaches were right over the trestle and the passengers couldn't get out."

"The trestle was over a big ditch, right?" he got the cleverness then and chortled, "They was trapped!"

"Yep. One by one, the three robbers, all wearing red bandanas and wielding rifles, corralled the train's crew — the engineer, the flagman, the fireman, the conductor, and the porter. Holding rifles at their heads, Rube forced them to collect jewelry and money from the passengers." Durwood paused to let the child's fantasy supply the details of dialog and action of that initial foray into outlawry. "So there you have it, the way it began. But something else interesting happened that day. The way I heard it, there was a detachment of AWOL soldiers being taken by six military policemen as prisoners to Forth Worth. Threatening to kill the conductor if the MPs did not cooperate, Rube disarmed them and told the soldiers, 'You can leave if you want to.' When they didn't respond, Rube cussed and called them sissies."

Jeremy digested that information and finally concluded that Rube had tried to be Robin Hood and got confused when rebuffed.

But he himself was not confused by the meaning of the agitated rocking of the chair as his mother exited it to disappear into the dark house with an angry swishing of skirts.

"I'm afraid we have offended the Mother," Durwood told his son, whose face was only a pale blob in the night.

"But why?" Jeremy asked, braking the foot that motored the squeaking swing.

"It's complicated, Son."

"But you will tell me the rest of the story, won't you?"

"We'll see. But now it's dark, and that means bedtime."

"Still no money for the electricity, Poppa?"

"I'm afraid not. But daylight will come before you know it, and by golly that light is free."

In the night, Jeremy awoke, sweating and needing to pee. Perched groggily on the commode, he was startled to overhear his parents' conversation in their room adjoining the bathroom.

His mother was clearly in attack mode, a fact that didn't surprise Jeremy since as far back as his memory reached, The Mother's existence could be defined as one long whine.

"I hate it here," she said bitterly, "and I want to go home."

Durwood's response was a tired sigh, as though he were reenacting an age-old battle. "It wouldn't be any better in Boston, Abigail. The Depression is everywhere."

Her tone became heavy with anger. "Don't talk to me like I'm an ignorant schoolgirl. You're not the only one in this family with an Ivy League degree."

Jeremy was familiar with this sally. Some uncanny insight made him understand the sarcasm attendant upon his mother's frustration with the failure of her professional aspirations. Beautiful and brilliant, she had earned a law degree, and in the process had fallen in love with Harvard's president of the Law Review, a charismatic Southern gentleman with aristocratic antecedents. In appearance, Durwood Upchurch was no Clark Gable, but he had a charm that could tame dragons. He had charmed his "damn Yankee" into marriage and brought her home to Linden, where the Depression trapped them.

"I'm so sorry, Abby." Durwood's remorse lay like a dull ache in Jeremy's chest. "I promised you paradise, but the Depression sabotaged our dreams. We will survive though. We have to be tough and patient with the times and keep on loving each other."

There was a reluctant softness in her reply. "I do love you, Durwood, but you're a dreamer, and you don't seem to understand that the world you grew up in as a descendant of Old South privilege is gone forever. And I have a hard time adjusting to a small town where there is no intellectual stimulation whatsoever, where my social life is limited to an anemic friendship with the town's only Jewish couple."

She paused and when she resumed, the sharp edge was back in her voice. "I know you're thinking that my unhappiness derives from superficial concerns, things that are a zero in the large scheme of things."

Jeremy shivered at the hint of sour vinegar in her next words. "Well, Durwood Upchurch, it's important to me to feel like, to be a human-being — not some brutalized, debased creature snorting and grubbing my way through life like a wretched farm animal." Suddenly, she sobbed, "My life is a bucket of shit."

Jeremy flinched at the shock of his refined mother's language. And Durwood was equally alarmed at the coarseness, never having heard his wife utter the word "outhouse," much less what went on in one. "Abby, this is not like you. What's come over you?"

"I'll tell you what's come over me. In a word, 'Rube Burrows.'" The name came out venomous and accusatory.

Durwood understood her lament, but Jeremy hadn't a clue. There he was, sitting perilously close to the edge of the commode seat in the dead of a hot night, listening to his distraught mother say "shit" like a regular old redneck and then blame it on Rube. He loved his mother, but he was infatuated by the legendary outlaw.

"Why do you object so strongly to my telling the story?"

"You are beguiling our son into idolizing a common criminal. And I will not have it, Durwood."

"Ah, Abby, you're making a mountain out of a molehill. Hearing the Rube story is a harmless solution to a young's boy's need for excitement and adventure. It's not like he's in danger of creating a graven image."

"Rube was a notorious outlaw, and he has an insidious clutch on Jeremy's imagination. He was a real person anchored in a real place with real people, and his dramatic death occurred on our street, two houses down from Jeremy's home. I love my son, and I can't sit by and see him corrupted by the allure of blazing guns and violence."

"Well, I don't want him to be warped by Puritanism and a Yankee pragmatism that destroys his imagination."

"And just what has imagination done for us lately?"

Durwood knew he was on spongy ground, but he plunged ahead. "You know the importance of the imagination, Abby. It's the wellspring of dreams, of creativity."

"Of course I understand. We'll just tell Jeremy to use his imagination and turn the molasses and biscuit into fillet mignon."

"Your sarcasm is unbecoming, Abby. You know that man does not live by bread alone."

"I know that the devil can quote scripture for his own purposes. Is it your absurd notion that we can live without bread?"

Durwood sighed, feeling himself to be on the precipice of defeat. "Of course not. I'm not so far removed from reality that I don't know we live in a time of hardship when bread is hard to come by, just to survive. But I think every civilized person knows it takes more than a belly full of bread to make life meaningful. I want my son's life to have a dimension enriched by an active imagination with all its possibilities for wonder and magic."

Abby cut him off. "Is that the source of your success? A rich fantasy life? Is that what you do every day, pretend to be a lawyer while actually wallowing in an orgy of psychic hedonism? Is that why we are destitute? With no client for two years?"

Smarting from her verbal razoring, Durwood asserted himself on a note of finality. "I am well aware of my shortcomings, Abigail, but I urge you not to deny Jeremy his home-grown myth, his harmless fantasy. We must not cheat him of a rich rewarding life. He is a good boy."

Jeremy's mother agreed, a tired little catch in her voice, and Jeremy imagined her curled up in his father's arms. His parents were at peace, and he was happy for them. He vowed to give up Rube and felt the pain of sacrificing a birthright.

But he reckoned without the power of the dark Rube factor in his blood. Stumbling back into bed, he plunged into a sleep of high adventure, where he rode with the Burrows gang, flinging bullets with wild abandon, yelling obscenities at cowering train crews, and riding hunched over the sweaty manes of gallant horses thundering through forests primeval with effete lawmen in hot pursuit. Astride his greathearted Silver, he thrilled at his self-image, a replica of Johnny Mack Brown, the famous Alabama football hero turned Hollywood cowboy star. Jeremy was soaring into a splendid kaleidoscopic scenario when a fickle imagination aborted the wild, free ecstasy with a rushing wind crying, "Just a bucket of shit, a bucket of shit."

He awoke then, and because he was a child, he did not try to analyze his dream, but the memory of it and his parents' passionate disagreement remained with him the rest of his life.

He never again mentioned the Rube story to his parents, but in spite of his vow, his imagination would not let it go. In his childhood, he mimicked the Rube persona with a distinct outlaw swagger, his hands in his pockets, and he often made a dramatic production of swooshing the saliva around in his mouth to generate a great glob of spit in what he thought was the Rube manner. When he was twelve, though, the memory was barely a footnote in his life. That changed, however, when he was sixteen and found a copy of a book about Rube on the coffee table at Aaron Bernstein's house. It caught his attention with the force of a slap, and his heart lurched at sight of a newspaper picture showing the dead outlaw in a pine box coffin propped upright to show the man's fabled pistols and his favorite Marlin rifle leaning against him.

While Aaron, his handicapped younger friend, napped, Jeremy read greedily, his passion reignited. The printed words lured him like the song of a Siren. He raced with the hunted outlaw, fleeing through the woods and swamps and caves of four states with the Southern Express Company detectives and scores of sheriffs bearing down on him. Jeremy's imagination invested the outlaw with the courage and doggedness of mythic noble animals grappling for life through the muck of the world's underbelly.

By the time the hunted man reached Marengo County in Alabama, Jeremy was at one with him, desperately trying to escape the clutches of the law and the relentless detective T.V. Jackson. Jeremy was with Rube when he read about the two black men, Jesse Hildreth and Frank Marshall, finding Rube asleep in a deserted cabin in Myrtlewood, overpowering him and turning him over to posse members John McDuffie and J.D. Carter. They brought him — shackled but defiant and joking — to the jail in Linden. There he was under heavy guard by the two Negroes and McDuffie, while Carter went to Glass's store across the street to phone G.W. Agee, chief of the Southern Express Company detectives, who was headquartered at Demopolis.

Rube entertained his captors with the skill of a court jester, often turning his predicaments into hilarity and beguiling his listeners with anecdotes about good deeds that humanized him.

"Folks think I got bushels of money," he said, "Ain't so. It comes and goes, and I'm happy to give it away. Take that time poor old Widow Burnett was getting tromped on by a lender threatening to foreclose on her place. When Pa told me 'bout that, it plum made me mad. So I give her the $160 she needed, and she made payment to that greedy old geezer. She had worried that she couldn't repay my money, but I told her not to fret, that I would get it back." He slapped his leg and straightened his back, enjoying his listeners' rapt interest. "And that's just what I done," he bragged. "When that bastard got to the woods a mile from her house, I was waiting for him on my horse with a bandana over my face and a pistol in my hand. It was like taking candy from a baby. He give up my $160 without a word." He chuckled at the memory of his foiling a perceived act of injustice. "They say you can't have your cake and eat it, too, but I know better."

His little audience was appreciative of the infamous man's wit and daring, but Rube was doomed, and Jeremy knew it. He felt no pity for the heavily bearded fugitive, whose filthy clothes hung loosely on his thin fame — only admiration for the wit and grit as Rube tricked his captors into abetting his escape. Pretending acute hunger, Rube persuaded them to give him his "grub sack," which contained some cookies and crackers. When he reached into the sack the second time, the cookie he brought out was a pistol loaded for death.

It was four o'clock in the dark of the October night when the desperate man rammed the gun into Jesse Hildreth's back and marched him across the street, directing him to call Carter out of the store with a ruse that McDuffie needed him at the jail. When the unsuspecting Carter stepped through the door, Rube threw his death threat into the violence-laden air.

"Give me my money and guns, Carter, or I'll blow your head off!"

Carter responded as if bested, "All right. I have your money in my pocket." When the money came from his hip pocket in the form of a .32 Smith and Wesson, it was a classic gun battle. When it ended, a bullet had pierced Carter's shoulder, and he was awash in blood. Rube, Jeremy's imaginary blood brother, lay dead in the street from Carter's fourth shot, which had cut the portal artery in his abdomen. Two brave and cunning men, one a law-abiding community leader and one an incorrigible desperado with bad-boy charisma, had dueled, and the rest was history.

At sixteen, Jeremy knew the difference between fantasy and reality, but reading the derring-do of the fatal gun battle catapulted him into the childish whim of "play like." He impulsively grabbed Ethan Bernstein's heavy shotgun from above the mantel, hoisted in to his shoulder, and pointed it at a startled Aaron, just entering the room.

In a convincing train-robber threat, Jeremy commanded, "Give me your money, or I'll blow your brains out."

Aaron laughed. "You'll never rob anybody with that gun. It's old as God."

It was then that the old hag, Destiny, stretched her shriveled arm upward, placed her bony fingers over Jeremy's hand and squeezed the trigger. Blood splattered, and Aaron went down like a limp rag doll on the Oriental rug.

Jeremy bolted, propelled by primal fear and confusion, his long legs gobbling up the mile to the railway depot, where a sluggish train labored to gather up speed for a long haul to Texas. With his knees almost failing him, he leapt into an empty boxcar. Sprawled on his back and assaulted by the barnyard smell of manure, he knew himself to be en route to hell.

It was the beginning of his journey on the rails as a hobo, his futile effort to disassociate himself from the guilt of having killed his friend. On that first day of his vagabondage, somewhere near Dallas, in the blackness of midnight, remorse and shame became his fellow travelers, and conscience rode shotgun on his shoulder. For an interminable time, this was his life, a twilight existence with a tormented mind and heart. He yearned for home and family, but he couldn't bear the thought of returning home as a prodigal son. So he rode the rails. Finally, he rode them into the bowels of World War II, succumbing to the summons of the eagle eyes and pointing finger of the "Uncle Sam wants you" poster.

And that purgatorial experience was a long jagged scar on his soul. His four-year redemptive saga began as newspaper headlines screamed "Day of Infamy," and a shocked world watched as demonic clouds mushroomed over Pearl Harbor. He joined the army with the notion that he might be able to atone for his sins through the noble effort to save his country.

The war, he came to feel, was a rape of humanity, a collage of suffering with no possibilities for hope and happiness. It was the savagery of boot camp, where he bled sweat and grew blisters on marathon missions for the love of country and for the respect of a drill sergeant, a cliché of military sadism, whom he loathed until the man embraced him in a bar and sang "God Bless America" with rivulets of tears testifying to his patriotism. It was mud, and blood, and guts on Normandy's shores, where thousands of fallen soldiers lay strewn on the beach like so much seaweed. It was a banshee wail encircling the whole world.

He met the violence head-on, inviting a death that would bring him peace. In orgies of angst, he charged from the foxholes pockmarking Europe, grinning into a grimace at his buddies' cursing. They called him Loco for his daring, reckless behavior in battle, not understanding why, across a continent, he defied the bullets that didn't want him.

His head became a zigzagging buzz of fragmented images

and memories: see Dick run, see Jeremy run, legs leaping over bodies, see Jeremy quarterbacking a grenade to his wide receiver, once upon a time there was a boy named Aaron who died strangling on bright red blood and the magnolia tree bloomed on and a machine gun is a friendly fellow if you love it, it will kill Germans Uncle Sam wants you but nobody wants a killer soldier wearing filth-stiffened fatigues reeking of urine and excrement staring at a bodiless arm reaching to pluck a blue wildflower standing pretty and proud in a heap of dung Ernie Pyle leaving his by-line on the face of history Rube hiding in caves and swamps what did he have to do with anything and Durwood and Abigail walking Puritan-proper across the street to church in the old courthouse from the halls of Montezuma to the shores of Tripoli a Nazi soldier with his German blond hair pedigree writhing in dying agony not knowing he was number twenty to die by Loco's gun and how many dead Nazi men equal one little Jew-boy dead in Alabama poor broken Poland its Auschwitz damned for the hollow-eyed apparitions that queued up waiting for the gas chambers to devour their race belly crawling in the battle but Rube didn't whine he would have guffawed at the muck of his life oh say can you see Sally Jane by the dawn's early light wearing pink and eyes shining at the box supper and dinner on the ground at the Methodist church what so proudly we hailed the warm Southern safety with guns outlawed weltanschauung the only German word Skeeter knew and never to know that it meant "world view" and not "go to hell" when he hurled the word at a German soldier and died for it at twilight's last gleaming life is a glitch a scarecrow a bucket of you know what hark the herald angels sing with no music but the zing of bullets to celebrate the birth of the Christ child crying in the snow of an alien land praying for one day of rest just one day remembering a girl's full inviting lips a dimple and teasing eyes wearing beauty like a queen over hill over vale we have hit the dusty trail and those caissons go rolling along where is my shepherd the one that promised I should not want Rube was generous gave his family land called the Flats Jeremy gave his family shame and heartbreak they called her Toyko Rose but she was Toyko bramble bitch rock of ages cleft for me lapping water like a dog from rain puddles eating c-rations made of desert dust let me hide myself in thee away from guilty as charged away from thou shalt not don't think about it think about the Jewish girl hiding in an abandoned barn somewhere in France black hair tangled and dark suffering eyes wild with terror Rube looked death in the face and mocked it Durwood Upchurch was a quiet man full of stories he was forbidden to share red is the color of blood, blood is the color of mortality and the bands played on with Harry James and Frank Sinatra making music to transcend the raucous roar of battle some said their star-dust melody could make you forget Jimmy Rawlings' head blown into smithereens the truth shall make you free that's a lie the truth is a German soldier run over by an American tank, squashed like a Goliathan roach where is your Aryan super race now Mr. dictator with your stupid moustache and your hair plastered down on your forehead yes Poppa I still have ole Rusty in my pocket mail call is another name for bitch with no little thin censored air mail letters for Loco Patton and Montgomery ego-racing to get to victory first what do they think this is some kind of crazy game with jowly Churchill and FDR refereeing the Mother has eyes so ocean blue you want to swim in them can you love me with blood on my hands and thorns in my heart Mother I'm sorry I wanted to be Rube Mother there are no mothers in the Ardennes Forest only soldier boys playing hide and seek with guns belching death to a Nazi army trying to hide in the forest and Brigadier General McAuliffe snarling "Nuts" at the German demand for surrender my country tis of thee sweet land of liberty and they called it the Battle of the Bulge and still he didn't die but the carpenter died on the cross and rose up and they called it Easter let the carpenter look on the killing fields in the Ardennes Forest see Uncle Sam's GIs kill the Nazi bullies like Hoss Agnew grabbing little Aaron's shriveled private parts in the rest room Jeremy dunking the

Hoss' head in the commode filled with excrement saving the Jew boy so he could later kill him with the blood so red on the pretty rug and ride the rails into the forest and see the Third Army play hero at Bastogne Rube's forests were pure and magical where has all the magic gone did it morph into Sieg heil the book said he was the Robin Hood of train robbers.

Then the war was over. Jeremy was in Reims, France, when Eisenhower's chief of staff and a general from the German High Command signed the terms of surrender in the allied headquarters in a red schoolhouse. On May 8, Jeremy and the entire free world celebrated V-E Day. A stunning French girl, her brown eyes ablaze with joy, grabbed him from the swollen crowd in the street, and he was thrilled at the softness of her young body. She led him into a cathedral, and in the yellow-blue flame from the candle she lit he looked for swastikas and pictures of a murdering Fuehrer. There was none. Instead, there was an awesome giant-sized icon of a risen Christ whose holy nail-scarred hands reached up into a brilliant sunburst of transcendent light. His heart soared as if the yoke of war had been lifted by the Prince of Peace.

"I'm going home," he said, and joined the jubilant military exodus back to America.

In Linden, he left the Greyhound bus and walked to Old Town, where he found his home deserted and locked. He set his bag down and eased onto the old swing. In wonder, he gazed at his mother's Lady Banks rose bush blooming in yellow joy like a fountain of flowers. Several cars passed with occupants staring curiously at the strange uniformed man sitting alone on the porch of an empty house. Eventually, one stopped.

He knew immediately that the man approaching him was Aaron Bernstein. The curly black hair, rebellious in the crew cut, was unmistakable, as was the limp bequeathed by polio. Shocked, Jeremy stood up, half expecting Rube, too, to swagger from Glass' store.

But there was no denying the reality of Aaron, his friend

from the age of innocence, as he clutched the still frail body in a bear hug. "You're alive!" he exulted. "How can you be alive?"

"I am alive because you were a terrible shooter, Jeremy Upchurch. Why did you think you could kill me when polio couldn't?" His hand went to his close-cropped curls in nervous pleasure.

"But you went down, and there was a river of blood," Jeremy protested.

"Just a shoulder wound, man. More damage to Mother's rug than to me. I figure I came out ahead — 4-F and Uncle Sam didn't want me."

"We sure could have used you."

"I knew you were there. In my gut I knew it."

They sat on the top porch step. "How could you be so sure?"

A little smile flitted at the corners of Aaron's mouth. "Remember Hoss and the toilet? Even back then, you were a teenage GI protecting a vulnerable Jew-boy from a redneck bully. Where else would you be but dealing death to the Nazi thugs that killed six million Jews?"

"Hitler was a black-hearted devil. I'm trying to purge him from my memory. But that's history. You've got to help me transition to the future."

"Well, that will have to come after you've reconnected with your past. Where do you want to start?"

The dread that had accompanied Jeremy throughout the trip home was like a drumbeat at the base of his skull. "Start right here where we used to play marbles in the front yard."

Aaron understood the implied question. "They're gone, you know."

"How gone?"

"Your dad is dead. Your mother has remarried and lives in Boston."

The silence bottled up in the cadaverous old house behind him bespoke a valley of dry bones, and Jeremy tried to feel something — anything. But he had killed too many. Ashes to ashes and dust to dust had been the bugle's command between reveille and taps of every day for three years. Now, death was not personal.

But it became personal with each step up the stairs to his father's office above the drugstore where Aaron took him. Durwood had left the office key with Aaron and had given instructions to make sure that Jeremy claimed his inheritance.

Opening the door was like opening a casket after a decade underground, with the hinges of the door squeaking in protest at the intrusion. Jeremy's memory came alive in the little room where Durwood had ostensibly practiced law. Mold and dankness and dust lay over everything like a pall, mutely beseeching not to be disturbed. A lone ray of sunshine gleamed brightly for a second on the Spartan furnishings dominated by a huge table-desk. Jeremy remembered how he and his father had built it using a cast-off wooden door and some rough-hewn legs. It was primitive carpentering, but Durwood had pronounced it "just right," and Jeremy sensed his father's ghost when the sunlight disappeared. But he had seen enough in that brief moment of light to know that the room had not been a law office but the retreat of a writer. For on the desk were dozens of neat stacks of handwritten journals. Jeremy looked at Aaron.

"When he knew he was going to die, he brought me up here. Said the only thing he wanted in his obituary was 'He lived to write books; then he died.' He wrote the books for you, Jeremy. They're your legacy."

Jeremy picked up the mildewed first volume and learned that the series of books was dedicated to him.

"It may seem like a strange inheritance," Aaron said, "but don't underestimate its worth. These are the original manuscripts. They've been published, and there's a small fortune in a bank account in your name. Look behind you."

Jeremy was impressed by the ten handsome volumes standing regally on the shelf. "This is incredible," he said.

"Your dad said something I didn't understand, something

about hoping that the books would help you to know how to handle the Rube factor. Do you know what he meant?"

"Kind of," he said.

Aaron left his friend alone with his space. No sooner had the door closed than Jeremy plunged into a two-day orgy of reading. It was an exhilarating odyssey as he accompanied his father through the pages. Durwood had retreated, crawling with courage back into his family's past, and chronicled their rise and fall from the time they left Ireland as peasants until the last old patriarch, Jeremy's grandfather, lost the Upchurch's little Black Belt kingdom to a clever and beautiful mulatto girl who had been kind enough to let him pay for Durwood's Harvard education. It was all there, painstakingly written with black ink in his father's neat handwriting, bold and vigorous in the early volumes and gradually becoming small and cramped in the final chapters.

Halfway through the saga, Jeremy stretched and took a break. He wrote and mailed a letter to his mother with plans for a visit. Then, on a whim, he caught a bus to Demopolis, where Rube Burrow's body had been autopsied, and continued by train on the route the dead outlaw's remains had traveled on that October tenth in 1890. The trip took him to Birmingham and from there to Sulligent, to Vernon, and finally to Fellowship Community, where an ancient overalled man pointed him in the direction of the cemetery. There he read the simple inscription: Rube Burrows 1855-1890. Without qualms, he followed the actions of other souvenir hunters by chipping off a small fragment of the marble tombstone.

Back at home, there was one thing left to do. He visited his father's grave and meticulously pulled up the tall grass growing in front of the tombstone. Then he pulled from his pocket two talismans — Ole Rusty and the Rube chip — which he placed on a ledge of the marker.

"Rest in peace, Poppa," he said. He let go of his own holocaust then and strode into the rest of his life with a tranquil heart.

Callie

My sister Callie was going to be a nurse. That's what she said when teacher asked us what we wanted to be when we growed up. She'd wrap her big feet around the shaky iron desk legs and say right out that she was gonna be a nurse and get folks like Nathan well when they got sick. Then she'd glare at the rows of good little girls who all wanted to be missionaries. Callie didn't care what they was gonna be, she was going to be a nurse and get sick folks well. She just hoped Nathan wouldn't die before she was growed enough to nurse him.

Callie was different. She was big, and her face was kinda yellow with funny looking places on it, and when she scratched, it left puffy looking streaks on the yellow. Her hair was about the color of sun-paled corn silks, and it was so straight it was always falling down over her eyes when she hung her head. She was so rough on clothes, Ma said, and made her wear overalls 'til she started getting a chest like the other girls. Then she looked funny in the feed sack dresses like she had been melted and poured in and was trying to get back out again. She wasn't fat, Callie wasn't, but she was big, and her legs looked like Nathan's with the white hairs crawling out around the freckles.

But Callie didn't care how she looked. She could do more than anybody else, and if they messed with her she'd show 'em, too. She showed Nelda Jenkins one time. Nelda spit on her when they were playing catch-the-fox, and Callie jumped on her and just about beat the hell out of her. And Callie just kept right on laughing and rolling Nelda in the red clay, rubbing her face in the ground and making her eat dirt. When teacher came out the back door and made 'em quit, Nelda cussed. She cussed Callie and she cussed the teacher. Callie just hung her head and fastened her overall strap. I remember the teacher made Nelda whup Callie with a switch, and we peeped in the window and Callie was laughing. She always laughed when she was mad. I guess teacher didn't like it when Callie didn't cry 'cause she took the switch and beat her till she was tired and Callie still didn't cry. She never did cry, not till she got to be a nurse.

I got mad 'cause teacher didn't whup Nelda, and I said, "It ain't fair. She oughta whupped Nelda too," and Cliff said, "She knows not to bother Nelda, or ole man Jenkins'll make her leave."

"But Nelda spit on Callie first," I argued.

Cliff looked down at me like I was dumb 'cause I wasn't as old as him, and he said. "That don't make no difference, Sam. There ain't no justice."

I guess he musta heard his Daddy say that. I didn't know what justice meant, so I hushed.

When Callie got a whupping at school, she got one at home, too. Always the kids that lived in the bottom would stop by our house and tell Ma if Callie was in a fight or anything. When Callie whupped Nelda, Ma took the razor strop and beat her till the blood oozed out around the whelps on her big legs and stuck the white hairs together. Ma grit her teeth and the knuckles on her red hands turned chalkish where she gripped the belt buckle, and she laid it on Callie, talking all the time. "Ain't I told you to leave that Jenkins gal alone? Ain't I told you? Say? Ain't you never gonna learn? Old man Jenkins'll be running us off if you don't leave his young'un alone. You know that, you know it. Why you keep messing with her? Why, why, why...." Ma screamed, crying and beating Callie, till she give out of breath. Ma didn't have much wind and that time she fainted and fell down. Callie just looked at Ma stretched out in the yard and kicked the dirt and watched the dust cake on Ma's arms and legs where they was sweaty. Callie just looked at her like she was disgusted and then walked off to the barn to see Nathan.

I dragged Ma to the chinaberry tree under the shade and got some water to bathe her face. She looked so pitiful in her greasy apron and kinda pretty like that. She was lots better looking than fat old Mrs. Jenkins even if she did have to pick cotton and chop stove wood. I thought Callie oughta wait on Ma if she was gonna be a nurse, but she never did. I guess it was because Ma didn't like Callie, not like she did me anyway. But Callie didn't care, she said so.

She didn't care about nothing, 'cept Nathan and nursing. When Nathan got sick, she wouldn't let nobody do anything for him 'cept her. She was his nurse. I guess, next to Nathan, Callie liked me best, 'cause she let me go with her and spend the night with him one time after he got sick. Nathan lived in the room next to the corn crib, and it was almost as nice as where we lived 'cept in the winter when it got muddy and smelled bad where the cows were. But I guess he liked it. He lived there ever since before I was born, Ma said.

The night we stayed with him, he said he was feeling kinda low. The board window was latched, and we shut the door behind us with a cross-bar. It was still daylight, but Nathan had the room shut up so the light wouldn't hurt his eyes. It was the first time I'd been in the room since he got sick and it was different. In the almost-dark you couldn't hardly see Nathan. His old iron bed was backed up in the corner, and it looked like the cobwebby shadows was eating him up. He had on his long johns and they was dirty yellow where the camphorated oil rags on his chest soaked through. His long brown hands kinda fooled with a hole in the quilt, and they looked like pieces of dried-up cowhide. Nathan was different in the bed. He looked mostly white with his silver hair plastered down across his forehead and his drooping mustache shining like cream. But I could tell it was him. The snuff dripped out of his mouth, and the brown juice matted the long ends of his mustache together and he had on his hat. It was a great black felt hat with a long brim that curled up like his mustache, and there was a little round hole in the top of it. Nathan never did pull his hat off, not even when he went to bed or to the table. I guess he was just old.

Callie set right in and started cleaning up. She swept the floor with the straw broom and covered up the basket full of half-shucked corn with some croker sacks she got out of the barn. Then she got the bowl from Nathan's bed and went to wash it, knocking the flies away from the dried egg yellow on the sides of it. I asked Nathan if he ate eggs at dinner too, and he said no, just at breakfast, and I wondered if maybe Ma forgot to take him some dinner. When I asked her the next day, she said he got plenty for a hired man.

Me and Callie built us a pallet on the floor next to Nathan's bed. The quilt we had over us was the one Ma used to wrap ice in and it stunk. When the red started coming in through the cracks in the logs, Nathan told Callie to open the window. He wanted to see the sun go down, and it made him sad because he said it looked like a man dying. Then it got dark and the crickets chirped and Callie started to light the lamp, but he said not to, it would spoil the effect. I guess he musta meant it wouldn't do no good to try to make the dead man come back alive.

Callie didn't talk much till I went to sleep, least till she thought I was sleeping. The quilt smelled so, and the mosquitoes hurt and I couldn't sleep. Callie slid off the pallet and squatted down by Nathan's bed and told him 'bout selling the boiled egg Ma fixed in her lunch to Mrs. Jenkins for some store candy, and they laughed together.

"If yore Ma found out, she'd lick the tar outa you, honey," Nathan said low, so as not to wake me up.

"I don't care. It don't hurt no longer than it lasts anyhow." Then the toughness sorta slid out of her voice. "But sometimes I want to cry."

Nathan's voice went soft. "How's that, Sis?"

"I just can't remember when it wasn't hard times. Seems like the only way I can stand it is to be hard myself." I couldn't believe what I was hearing, but I felt the same as Callie when she asked, "Is it ever going to end, Nathan?"

"I won't see it end, but you will. Things have to get better, and you'll be all right. You'll be a nurse like you always wanted." His voice dropped into a cough.

"I ain't never gonna be no nurse," Callie said, and I could hear her foot pushing at the floor. "We ain't got no money, and Ma wouldn't let me if we did."

Nathan moved over to the side of the bed so he could see Callie sitting on the floor. "Yore Ma ain't got nothing to do with it." Then he waited a long time, and finally he said, "When I die I don't want you to let nobody else touch me."

The shuck mattress crackled in the dark, and I could feel him pushing hisself up in the bed. "Looka here," he whispered raspingly, "here it is. Put yore hand up here and feel the money. Feel that wad? When I die don't let nobody in here till you get it. You here?"

"Yeah, Nathan," Callie whispered as she slid back on the floor. "I'll hide it so she can't find it."

I thought Callie oughta tell him he wasn't gonna die, but I guess she knowed he was. She was a natchel-born nurse. For a long time they didn't say nothing, and Nathan kept breathing through his mouth real loud.

Nathan was dead the next morning. His head in the black hat was jammed back against the iron bedstead, and his eyes stared blind at the ceiling. His tongue was big and hanging out and ants were crawling around on the dried snuff on his mustache. I looked at him and got sick. Callie made me go out, and she put the bar across the door after me. She stayed in there all day, and she wouldn't come out when Ma and Grandma come to lay him out. When the sun started down, she opened the window, and at dark she come out and she had the black hat. She had it and we never did see it again, not till she got to be a nurse.

Callie was kinda mixed up from then on, and she had a hard time growing up. She was strong as an ox and stubborn as a mule and everybody said she was mean. But she wasn't lazy and she worked. After school she picked cotton for Mr. Ted, and he gave her fifty cents for every hundred pounds she picked. Then she'd come home after dark and hunt the cows and get water from the spring. In the summer she worked in the fields like a man. We had to have a crop or Mr. Jenkins would run us off, and we didn't have no place to go, especially since Pa was off working with the CCC. He couldn't help it, Ma said. I remember seeing him one time when he come home. I didn't like him.

Then Callie went off to school. I remember the morning she left. The black and red store-bought dress stretched across her belly like a drum, and her patent leather shoes cracked across the toes. Ma had rolled her hair up in corn shucks, and the heavy streaked mass twisted around her head, making her look like a porcupine. Her skin was dark brown from the sun, and the white hairs on her arms and legs stood out like bristles; you could see the white strip across her shoulder where the cotton sack hung. The last time we seen her she was walking down the road, swinging the big suitcase with a rope around the middle to keep it from coming open.

The wash-out between the house and the road was just a ditch then. It growed to be a gully before Callie come back again.

It wasn't much different at home when she come back, 'cept for Ma being dead and Grandma and her walking stick living with me, and the gully being bigger. It was August and so hot the house's tin top cracked under the sun, and flies wiggled on their bellies. It was laying-by time, and the evening Callie come home I was stretched out on the porch, watching Grandma churn. She always shooed the flies when she churned, but she forgot to shoo when she looked up and seen the woman open the gate. She looked hard, her eyes opening wide out of the wrinkles, but she couldn't figure out who it was. I knowed it was Callie.

I guessed she was a lady too. She wasn't big any more, and she didn't push her feet along the ground. She walked up the dirt path kinda slow and easy like a lean yellow cat, and she didn't hang her head either. She had on a blue dress and it made the sky around the sun come sliding down, and it looked soft and cool around her. When she come to the chinaberry tree, she reached up and pulled off a handful of leaves, and the full rounded curve of her breasts pushed against the soft dress. Her hair was short, and she had it combed back from her face. Any fool could tell she wasn't hard to look at.

She come up on the wooden steps, and Grandma said, "Well, if it ain't the old cow." Callie kinda smiled a little around the lips. And her eyes stayed blue like the sun shining through water on a knife blade. She hugged us both, and I could feel how hard she was.

I put her suitcase with the initials on it in the front room and then we talked till sundown. She told us she was getting a week off to rest, then she'd go back and graduate in three months. She was going to do some special studying about babies and then go to work in a hospital and just work with babies all the time. She liked babies.

Callie didn't talk much anytime, 'cept maybe to say pass me something at the table or ask about something that had happened while she was gone. Grandma didn't know exactly what to make of her not talking and all. She liked to talk to herself.

I couldn't figure out what she come back for. Nobody asked her. So far as she knowed, nobody cared whether she ever come back or not. But she stayed.

Then one night when the mosquitoes was holding revival meeting so loud nobody could sleep, Ellis come and said Eunice was sick and would Grandma go set with her till he could get the doctor from town. She was in a pretty bad fix, Ellis said. Thought it was appendicitis.

"Appendicitis," Grandma snorted, feeling the wall for the nail where her clothes was hanging. "What the fool needs is a midwife." She kept fussing in the dark, trying to get her dress over her head. I don't know if Callie had even been to bed or not. When I got my overalls on and found Grandma's walking stick, Callie was waiting in the door. She had on her uniform, and she looked so clean and white I cussed out loud. If she stayed here long, she wouldn't be so pretty and white. But I couldn't tell her nothing.

She was a nurse.

It was two miles in the swamp to Ellis' house and it wasn't easy walking. Even in the dark you could feel the heavy dust lying still like in the air, and there wasn't a sign of a moon. It was hilly, and the gutted road was rough, but Callie stayed ahead, and her white heels come down hard on the sliding rocks. Grandma grunted and talked. Eunice oughta have to suffer, Grandma said. Anybody that'd run off and leave a house full of young'uns and traipse all over the country with any man imaginable... God oughta let 'em die. Eunice had her belly full of nerve, come poking back here, big round as a cow. She talked on and on, allowing as how she couldn't tolerate such fool trashy women.

Then she hushed, and you couldn't hear nothing 'cept our feet in the ruts and the parched clay cracking under our shoes. Now and then stunted pine trees made a dark, withered outline on the ditch bank.

"Ain't never seen such a black night in August since here I been," Grandma said. "Plague take the devil," she kept saying, "plague take it."

But that didn't help none, 'cause there still wasn't a breeze, just hot lightning bugs and warm dusty air coming up from the baked ground. I knowed it wasn't all that hot for August, but I could feel the sweat run down my legs, and it tickled where the wet made grooves in the caked dirt around my ankles.

Callie kept on walking, faster and faster, and finally we got to the top of the hill where you could look down and see the light from the house at the bottom. The dark path was so gully-washed I just about had to tote Grandma, but Callie kept right on like she knowed just how deep every ditch was, and I thought about all the times she used to hunt the cows after dark.

The house looked like it was a long way off till we got right up on it. It squatted, so close on the ground that a dog couldn't get under it without scratching his back. Everything was so quiet and still in the dark it seemed like we was slipping up on the barbed wire fence, and when Callie opened the gate, you couldn't hear anything but the screeching of the wire over the nail. There wasn't any trees or grass 'cause it was bottomland, and they had a plank across the yard to the doorstep to walk on. When Callie stepped on the hiked-up end of the plank, a dog, with its head stuck out from under the porch, sniffed and barked short in his sleep. Somebody on the porch said, "Shut up, Mary," real low, and when Callie got to the big rock that was the doorstep, a long barefoot boy with his hands in his baggy overall pockets moved into the strip of light from the door. He just stood there looking like a dried-up prison guard in the yellow light. I knowed he was trying to figure out who Callie was. She didn't move, so I said, "Evening, Haskie." When he finally made out who we was, he said, "Evening, Mr. Sam. Y'all come on in," and followed us into the room.

Callie must not remembered how it was. She kept looking and looking. The floor sunk in the middle, there was big cracks in the wall, and they had a quilt stuck in the window where a pane was out. The fireplace looked like a hog wallow, with the hicker-nut hulls and ashes all over the cracked bricks. It was always like that. The twisted fly-specked mirror made the dresser look like it had a broken neck, and the doily on the mantle was dirty and ragged. It was dark in the kitchen, and all you could see was the stove and its rusty pipe going up through the tin top.

The kids all looked alike, so dirty and hungry-eyed it was a sin. Haskie was mighty friendly, but I wouldn't trust a one of them further than I could spit. I couldn't ever remember which was the oldest, Haskie or Sally Mae. I guess it was Sally Mae. When we come in, Callie looked at Sally Mae over in the corner holding the last young'un. She was a thin girl, with big breasts and lips that turned down. Grandma said she was no count. Too many men in pretty cars come to see her.

The cross-eyed twin boys were the ones that did the work of the farm, and I guess the only decent ones in the lot. They was propped against their half full cotton sacks behind the dresser, their crooked eyes staring up at us and their mouths opening in sleepy, twisted grins.

A tired-looking little girl in a dirty underskirt fired the smoke bucket in a corner by the sickbed. Pot-bellied mosquitoes swarmed, and Callie rubbed her eyes when a big gust of smoke filled the room, making the yellow light turn gray.

"How's your ma?" Grandma asked.

"I don't know, Miz Sally; she's been moaning like that a long time," Haskie answered her.

Grandma laid her walking stick down and walked over to the bed, her old eyes squinting down at Eunice. She slid her hands over the heavy breasts, then felt the great bulge under the sheet. Callie watched her, and she watched the young ones staring. They grinned, shamefaced. Callie looked at 'em, and then she went and slung the smoke bucket out of the window. When she turned around, they stopped grinning.

"You'd better get the kids out," she told me. They got up and went out on the porch, and I latched the door after them.

"What about you?" she asked me.

"Think I'll stay," I told her. I didn't like the way she sounded so bossy.

"Suit yourself," she said, twisting her shoulders and listening to the low, bubbling sound from the bed. That's the way it started, a low bubbling sound from way down in the throat, and it kept boiling up and up till the long high scream beat down hard on our heads. I followed Callie to the bed, and when I put my hands on the iron bedstead, pieces of blue cracked paint fell down on Eunice's greasy, gray-brindle hair. Callie put her hands on Eunice's forehead, and the woman opened her eyes.

"Well, bless my soul and body," she said, her jaws sagging. "It's Callie Ford."

"Yes, it's me," Callie said.

"Guess everything'll be all right now. Ain't never had a shore 'nough nurse to wait on me before." She kept talking and kinda grinning while Callie pulled down the sheet. She had on a coarse cotton gown, and her body spread all over the bed. Callie took the hot smoothing iron wrapped up in rags from her side and handed it to me. I went to the fireplace and put it down.

Callie said low, "When you going to stop having babies, Eunice?"

Eunice was breathing hard and jerky, straining to raise her glob of fat up in the bed. The pains caught her, and her face looked like wet ash.

Callie looked at her watch and put her hand on the mound of belly.

"I ain't gonna have no baby," Eunice said.

Callie motioned me to come help her, and she told the woman it wouldn't be long now. We took her out of bed, and there was a huge wet spot on the sheet. I thought about that hot iron he had had in the bed and figgered she had done a lot of sweating. But Callie said, "Her water's broke."

"I ain't gonna have no baby," Eunice gasped. "I ain't gonna have no baby."

Callie told her she was going to have that baby, whether she wanted to or not, that she meant to see to it that the baby was born. She propped up the woman's legs and told me to keep them steady while she examined her. She didn't need a tape measure to know how dilated she was.

"I guess we'd better fire up the stove for some hot water. Right?" She nodded, and I was glad to get away from the screaming.

"Bear down, Eunice. Push hard. It's coming."

Bringing the water, I watched Callie's hands, long and white, pushing up the wobbly legs and reaching in for the baby. She talked to the woman, and her voice was like her hands, willing the baby to be born.

Callie smiled. Smiled kinda glad-like with the sweat running off the sides of her face as her hands come around the baby's head, its shoulders, and finally its long legs. It was a yellow, shriveled up thing, but Callie's hands loved it.

At first I couldn't make out if she was laughing or crying, but when she moved over to the broke dresser mirror with the baby, the cracked glass and dirt faded, and I could see her face was shining with the crying kind of wet. My sister Callie never did cry. Not till she got to be a nurse.

It come to me then, kinda strange like, that the Depression was over.

Betty Jean Tucker was born in 1931, the very heart of the Great Depression, in the little farming and sawmill community of Octagon in Marengo County, Alabama. For the first ten years of her life, she experienced the Depression up close. Though she was only a child then, the cataclysmic era seared into her memory a dark record of life in that time and place. Moreover she has drawn on years of narrative handed down by relatives and friends to enrich the fictional stories in On a Darkling Plain.

The author at age 19, when "Callie," the first of the *Plain* stories, was published.

At age 83, she enjoys retirement and is still passionate about writing.

The author has lived in the Alabama Black Belt town of Linden except for college years at Alabama College (now the University of Montevallo) and a brief stint as a reporter for the *Birmingham Post-Herald*. With a Ph.D. from the University of Alabama, she chaired the Division of Languages and Literature at the University of West Alabama for twenty years and is now retired.